Abigail

By C.J. Whitcomb

Cover art by © Andrey Kiselev and © samiramay and licensed by J.C. Everlyn through Adobe Stock (https://stock.adobe.com)
Edited by © J.C. Everlyn

Description

When a man is murdered by a secret society, it's up to his vampire daughter to avenge him. Along the way, she discovers a world of blood, sex, death, and darkness. Twists, turns, and mysteries await her around every corner.

A special thanks to….

My editor J.C. Everlyn, my friends and family for the support and encouragement you give.

Also, thank you to my readers, I hope you enjoyed this book….

Contents

Chapter One

Paris, France, October 16th, 1793. While many people of France are mourning the loss of the beloved Marie Antoinette, others are celebrating her execution at Place De La Concorde.

On the other side of the river, there's a grand ball taking place at the Hotel De Salm. The hotel is beautiful and had finally opened its doors three years earlier after nearly a decade of construction.

In the ballroom, the string band plays, and the attendees are mingling with their drinks in hand. The doors swing open and a beautiful young woman enters. The music stops, and everyone in the room turns to face the young auburn-haired woman in her infinite beauty. Only one man in the crowd is brave enough to approach. He extends his arm, taking her hand in his and leans over to gently kiss her knuckles.

"Good evening madam, I am Jacque Bisset. It's a pleasure to have you grace us with your presence on such a splendid occasion. Would you care to dance?"

"I'm Abigail, and I would love to dance, but it seems the band has stopped playing," replies the young woman.

Jacque raises his right hand, signaling the band to begin playing as they were before. This time the music was a soft romantic melody that would almost carry you across the dance floor without ever lifting or moving your feet.

Abigail and Jacque glide across the floor like two lovers dancing in the sheets. Everyone in the room watches them as if it's the first time witnessing such a perfect display of beauty radiating from the two of them. Jacque gestures to the crowd instructing they all mind their business and dance.

Abigail whispers into his ear as she rests her head on his shoulder.

"I have always been intrigued by a man who can command a room."

"And I, madam, have always been fascinated by a woman who can get everyone's attention just by walking through the door. Tell me, Abigail, what brings you to my party tonight?"

Abigail moves her head and places it on Jacque's other shoulder; she again whispers in his ear. "I came to kill a vampire."

March 6, 1792. Abigail is awoken by the sound of two men arguing. She sits up in bed and stands to her feet. Then quickly strips off her white nightgown that's form-fitting and drapes down to her ankles. On most other days, she would wait for her housemaid to come into her room and help her dress, but on this day, Abigail is in a rush and dresses herself.

She leaves the room, heading down the hallway of her family's mansion and descends the staircase. Her father, Francois Cariveau, is standing in the foyer arguing with Jean Baptiste Devereux, the patriarch of another prestigious family who runs in the same social circle as the Cariveaus. The argument had stopped just as she came down the stairs.

She had missed what was said, and Jean Baptiste stormed out. Her father slams the door shut behind him.

"Father, what was that all about? Who was that man, and why would he be yelling at you?"

"That's nothing a young girl should concern herself with on the first day of her eighteenth year. Now come with me. I have something for you."

She follows him into the living quarters and over to a small desk he had built for her when she was a child. He pulls open the top drawer and reaches in, removing a small handcrafted wooden box. He hands the box over to his beautiful daughter; she opens it and removes a cross necklace.

"I know it's not very visually pleasing, but you never know it may save your life one day." Says Francois.

"What's it made out of? It's really heavy."

"It's a family heirloom that has been passed down from generation to generation, starting with your great grandmother,

Pearlina. Forged in fire from the strongest wrought iron, it will provide you with protection against the evils of the world."

"What are these evils that you speak of?" She asks

"Let's hope you never have to find out," he hugs Abigail and plants a kiss on her forehead.

"Must you go out tonight, father? It is my birthday after all, and you've not been around much these last few months."

"Yes, my dear Abigail, I must, but I'll be back in time to celebrate this momentous occasion. After tonight our lives will be forever changed."

She hugs her father, wrapping her arms around his bloated waist. A loud knocking echoes from the front door of the Cariveaus' home. Their butler, Ansel, who had been like a member of the family, opens the door and greets the visitor. An older gentleman with a long riding crop tucked underneath his armpit stands on the stoop of the home.

"How may I help you, kind sir?" Asks Ansel.

"I'm here to drive a Miss Cariveau around and take her wherever she may want to go."

"And who sir shall I say has sent you in their name?"

"I believe he told me his name was Devereux. Thibauld Devereux."

"Very good sir," Ansel responds. "I'll send her out right away." He shuts the door.

A few short minutes tick by when the door reopens, and Abigail, in a beautiful violet evening gown, emerges from the home. Her father, Francois, escorts her gracefully down the three cement steps of the stoop and helps her into the horse-drawn carriage that is awaiting her. The driver boards the carriage and prompts his horse to start trotting. Meanwhile, her father flags down another carriage heading in the opposite direction. He climbs aboard and turns his head to look back at his lovely daughter, who, as of today, is a woman.

Francois sits silently for the entire carriage ride until he reaches his destination. He then climbs down from the carriage and tips his driver. The driver pulls away as Francois turns to approach the front door of the Devereux abode. He knew that Jean Devereux's son, Thibauld, would be meeting up with Abigail while he and Jean have a sit-down. He knocks on the door and is greeted by the Devereux's newest maid Marie, who is also Jean's latest plaything. Marie leads Francois up the stairs and into a large room with a long wooden table in the center. A beautiful tight bodied woman dances on the tabletop. Completely nude, she moves her body seductively like a snake moves to the sound of a flute. Several men sit around the table, watching her every move as if they were hypnotized. These eight men were the leaders of different factions all over Paris that formed the secret society known only to a select few. The members referred to their organization as *The Order of The Black Veil.*

It was unknown what the Order stood for or even how it got started. All anyone really knew was not just anyone could join. Becoming a full-fledged member was the reason Francois is sitting with such an elite group of men this very night.

"Are you ready to become one of us, Mr. Cariveau ?" Asks Devereux who is in charge of the entire fraternity.

"I've never been more ready for anything in my life." He answers with overwhelming enthusiasm.

Jean nods toward one of the members at the end of the table. The man stands up from his chair and points to the door instructing the nude woman to leave the room. As she closes the door behind her, another member stands and approaches Francois, removing a black handkerchief from his jacket pocket. Francois bows his head ever so slightly, allowing himself to be blindfolded.

"I believe you know what to do now," Jean says.

Francois strips completely nude. The two standing members guide him to the long wooden table. He lays down on his back with his face toward the ceiling of the room. The fraternity all stand taking positions around the table and Francois. Jean gets in close and leans down. He places his hands on Francois's thigh, then sinks his sharp fangs into the flesh of his legs. Everyone follows the lead, and one after another, they sink their teeth in. Francois sweats as his skin is penetrated. He shivers, feeling cold as the blood is slowly drained from his body. His vision blurs as his best friend, Paulo, kisses his neck before taking Francois's life force into his mouth and letting it drip down his throat.

Halfway across town, Abigail ascends a staircase being careful not to slip on the rose petals that are covering the steps. The carriage driver had brought her to the Notre Dame Cathedral. When she reaches the roof, Thibauld greets her, handing her a single red rose.

"Thibauld Devereux, why have you brought me here?"

"Dear sweet Abigail. You're a woman now. I wanted to ask for your hand in marriage before anyone else could."

"But why would you want to marry me, we don't know each other at all. You've only just moved back from London two weeks ago before that I hadn't seen you since you were a sickly little boy who couldn't even get out of bed. When you moved away, everyone thought you had died."

"Well, as I stand here before you on this beautiful night, you can see that I did not succumb to my illness."

Thibauld reaches for her hand, but she pulls away.

"I'm sorry, but I won't marry anyone without first speaking to my father."

"Who do you think came up with the idea? Has no one told you about this?"

"Told me about what exactly?"

"Sweet innocent little Abigail, when you're born into a family as prestigious yours or mine, more often than not, the patriarchs of both families will get together and arrange for their children to be married. It's how the rich and powerful stay rich and powerful."

Thibauld reaches out again, this time grabbing Abigail by the wrist. She tries to pull away, but his grip is too tight.

"Let's not do this. Our fathers made a deal, and it's up to us to see it through."

"Listen to me, Thibauld Devereux. I will not marry a man that I am not in love with regardless of who makes a deal with my father," she says, using all of her strength to break free of his grip.

Without warning, he raises his hand and brings it down, slapping her across the lips. She's stunned; blood trickles from a small cut on her bottom lip. He grabs her by her neck and pulls her in close, pressing his lips against hers; he tastes her blood before pushing her off of the roof of the cathedral. He watches from the ledge as her body falls to the streets below.

Chapter Two

Abigail lays lifeless on the street. Blood pours from the wound in the back of her head, caused by the impact of her fall. A hooded figure is walking by but stops and kneels next to her. The figure picks her up and carries her away through the darkness of the night.

The following morning Abigail wakes up to sunlight shining through the window. She looks around, realizing she's in her own bed but has no memory of returning home the night before. Her violet dress is draped over a chair in the corner. Still, in her nightgown, she leaves the room and descends the stairs.

"Father. Are you home?" She calls out.

Ansel appears just at the bottom of the steps as she makes her way down.

"Oh, Ansel, have you seen my father?"

"No madam, I fear I have not. Until this very moment, I was unaware you were here."

Several loud knocks echoed through the door. Ansel opens it.

"Inspector Laurent, what brings you here?" Abigail asks as Gabriel Laurent enters the foyer.

Gabriel removes his hat and holds it to his chest, "Madam Cariveau, I am sorry to have to be the one to tell you this, but your father's body was found this morning."

Abigail feels her knees go weak, and the devastating thoughts of losing the man who had raised her causes her to lose control of her body; her legs give way. Ansel grabs her mid-fall and helps her regain her stance, and she looks at Gabriel. "It cannot be true," she says. "It mustn't be him. I demand you take me to see the body you claim is my father."

"I'm not sure that's an entirely good idea, Miss Cariveau."

"Get your carriage ready, and I will meet you outside. You're taking me to see his body."

Gabriel looks toward Ansel inquisitively.

"I suggest you listen to her inspector, I knew her mother, so trust when I tell you, hers is not a wrath you want to face," says Ansel.

Gabriel says nothing as he turns and walks outside to wait. Abigail walks upstairs to her room to get dressed.

Gabriel stands by his carriage, watching as the people of the city walk by. He hears the door of Abigail's home open behind him. As he turns his head toward the sound, his jaw nearly hits the pavement when he sees her step out in a forest green dress and a small hat to match. He is immediately taken aback by how beautiful she is. He stammers over his own words as he opens the carriage door.

"Right this way, madam," Gabriel says as he helps her in.

"Thank you, inspector Laurent." She replies, taking a seat.

Gabriel climbs into the carriage and sits opposite of Abigail, then signals the driver to take off. As the carriage bounces and the horses pull away, Abigail looks the inspector in his eyes.

"I know you're wrong," she says.

"I beg your pardon, Miss Cariveau."

"The body you found isn't my father. It can't be."

"How can you be sure of that?"

"I don't know. I just have to believe it's not."

Gabriel tries to hide his facial expression, but still, it displays concern for Abigail's naive young mind. The carriage driver turns his head slightly and shouts toward Gabriel.

"We're here, inspector." He says.

Thank you, Clive." He replies. "Looks like we'll have to walk from here, Miss Cariveau."

He helps Abigail exit the carriage.

Place De La Concorde is full of people, and there's no way for a carriage to drive through. Gabriel Laurent locks arms with Abigail and guides her through the crowd. Pushing their way through the citizens, Gabriel and Abigail reach the obelisk. There at the bottom are her father's remains. She's in shock, gazing at her father's body. She can tell his blood had been completely drained. The bloated waist she had her arms around the night before is now thinned. She steps closer and notices the tiny puncture wounds all over his naked corpse. She almost locks eyes with her father's as they are still open, but before she does, a hooded figure stands in the crowd on the other side of the obelisk. A flash of memory from the night before disrupts her thoughts.

She remembers waking up in a dark room, she's dazed and tries to speak. The hooded figure standing over her puts his finger over her lips, and shushes her. The memory ends there.

The hooded figure turns around and makes his way through the crowd. Abigail follows, she pushes her way passed the bystanders but is knocked down, losing the hooded stranger.

Gabriel rushes to her side, helping her to her feet.

"Miss Cariveau, are you okay?" he asks. "Why did you take off like that, and who was that hooded person?"

"I'm not sure, but I feel like I know them, I have a memory of them, though I'm not sure when or where we would have met."

"Well, nevermind that now, let's get you home. You've had a very trying day already, and it's not even noon."

Gabriel once again locks arms with her and guides her back to the carriage, they climb in and head back to her home.

Abigail is upstairs in bed and is physically and mentally exhausted, still trying to wrap her head around the death of her father. Ansel and Gabriel are in the living room downstairs.

"So inspector, what do you think happened to her father?" Ansel asks.

"Mr. Cariveau's body was covered in small puncture wounds. We believe it to be the result of an attack, most likely rodents, maybe bats."

"That's odd, don't you think?"

"Well, it's not common."

Ansel stands, indicating to the inspector that it is time for him to leave.

"Thank you, inspector. Please be sure to keep us informed if you find out anything else."

"Will do. In the meantime, you be sure to take care of that girl upstairs; you're the only one she has left."

Ansel nods in acknowledgment while walking Gabriel to the door and showing him out. Shutting the door behind Gabriel, he turns and stands at the bottom of the stairs. Looking up toward Abigail's room, he promises himself to always look after her and do whatever it takes to keep her safe.

Chapter Three

At sunset, Abigail wakes up to the sound of Ansel entering her room with a tray of food.

Groggy, she opens her eyes, "What's this?" she asks.

"Just some warm milk and a plate of crackers, I thought you could use something to eat."

"Thank you, Ansel. That's very kind of you, but now that my father's dead, there's no need for you to be here."

"Begging your pardon, Miss, but your mother and father hired me to take care of you not to take care of them. Over the years, I've grown to think of your family as my own. From where I'm standing young lady, this is the time you need me more than ever, and with all due respect, I'm not going anywhere."

"Ansel, you're too good to me sometimes."

Ansel smiles and then turns to take his leave, but then pauses and faces her once more.

"There's something I feel I should tell you, Miss, but I'm not sure I know how to say it," he admits.

"It's okay you can talk to me about anything, just sit down and start from the beginning," Abigail replies while gesturing towards the chair in the corner of the room.

Ansel takes a seat.

"Okay, here goes. When your father first hired me to look after the house, everything was perfectly normal. I was to do the cooking and cleaning, of course and was expected to mind my own business. That all changed when your father found out your mother was pregnant with you. There were no problems with the pregnancy itself, but during childbirth, something went horribly wrong. While your mother was in labor for several hours, breathing in and out and trying to push, she finally delivered you, and then she stopped breathing herself. There was so much blood loss nobody knew what to do. The midwife placed you in your father's arms and covered your mother with the bloody sheet. Your poor father was devastated. At least until a doctor friend of his arrived and instructed everyone to leave the room, this included you and your father."

Ansel takes a moment to observe Abigail's reaction. She is sitting there listening intently, so he continues.

"Moments later the doctor exits the room and tells your father, he may go in to see his wife. Naturally, your father was curious as to exactly what happened, he wouldn't let his friend leave until he got some answers."

"What were the answers?" asks Abigail.

"I'm not sure, but I do know he gave your father this address," Ansel says while reaching into his pocket.

He pulls out an old piece of paper that is ripped in some places and wrinkled in others, and he hands the paper to Abigail.

"Maybe we can go there and get some more information," Ansel suggests.

"No. You stay here I'll do this on my own. Don't worry; I'll be back shortly."

Abigail stands up from the bed, and Ansel leaves so she can change into something more appropriate.

Later that evening, Abigail stands in front of a building that looks as though it was abandoned in mid-construction. She checks the addresses next to the door then checks the slip of paper in her hand.

Entering the building with curiosity and caution, it's dark inside, but Abigail has no trouble seeing as she walks around. It felt so natural that she didn't even notice her ability to see through the dark.

There wasn't much inside the building to look at other than some bookshelves and some old books written by Donatien Alphonse Francois, more commonly known as the Marquis De Sade.

Abigail picks up a book titled, *La Philosophie Dans Le Boudoir* (The Philosophy of the Bedroom). A folded piece of paper from inside the book falls to the floor and unfolds as it touches the ground. Abigail doesn't pick it up, but her eyesight amplifies like a magnifying glass zooms in. It's a list of eight names, and at the top of the list is written *Black Veil Members.*

Abigail picks up the note and the book and returns home a short time later. Upon entering the house, she goes straight to Ansel's sleeping quarters.

"Ansel, Ansel, come quick!" Abigail yells as she bangs on his door.

Ansel opens the door in a panic.

"What's going on, Miss? What troubles you?" He asks.

"I went to the address you gave me, when I got there I could tell the room was dark but I could see everything clearly. As I continued looking around, a piece of paper dropped on the floor, and I could read it without picking it up. What is happening to me, Ansel? Something is very different. These changes are unnatural, and they're scaring me."

Ansel wraps his arms around her and guides her to the living room and helps her sit on the couch.

"You just sit down right there, Miss, and I'll make us some tea, then I'll get us each a cup and explain everything I can to the best of my ability."

Moments later, Ansel returns to the living room. Abigail reaches out and takes her cup from his hand. He sits down and sips his tea before beginning to explain.

"The iron necklace that your father gave you yesterday, do you still have it?" he asks while looking at Abigail.

She feels around her neck. "No, it's gone. I swear I never took it off after he placed it on my neck."

"I was afraid that might be the case. How much did your father tell you about the necklace?"

"Not very much at all, just that it was passed down from generation to generation."

"Yes, that's correct, it was given to your great grandmother, Pearlina. I'm not sure why it was given to her or by whom, but I do know it's made from the strongest iron the people in her village could dig up."

"What village was she from?" asks Abigail.

"Versailles. It was established in the 1600s. I'm sure you've heard of it. It's not far from here; only it's grown so much, it's now considered a city."

"It sounds beautiful," she replies.

"That it is, Miss. Nevertheless, this necklace was given to her to provide her with protection from the evils of the world. No one really knew what that actually meant, but years later, Pearlina died while giving birth to your grandmother, Agatha. Then when Agatha became older, she was sold to a workhouse, and the master got her pregnant. She gave birth to your mother, Collete, but was forced to give her away or lose her life. Pearlina passed down the necklace as protection. Agatha placed it around your mother's neck before she gave her away, and she wore it until the day you were born."

"If the wrought iron necklace was meant to provide them with protection from the evils of the world. Why did Pearlina and my mother die giving birth?"

"I'm getting to that. I wasn't completely honest with you earlier. I know more than I said I did. When your father pulled the doctor to the side to talk, the doctor handed him the necklace. He told your father the necklace was created to repress Pearlina's inner self."

"What do you mean by that?" Abigail asks, sipping her tea.

"The women in your family were all born with what some would call an affliction. I call it a gift. A gift that remains dormant until the eighteenth year unless repressed by an object blessed by a holy man."

"Like the cross my father gave me?"

"Exactly. Do you recall how you lost it?" Ansel asks.

"No." She replies.

A flash of memory enters her mind. Abigail sees herself falling off the roof. The memory changes to the hooded stranger standing over her and pulling the necklace off of Abigail's neck, throwing it to the street.

"Someone took it from me last night," Abigail says as the flash of memory stops.

"I see." Ansel says, "that explains the new ability to see in the dark and amplifying certain things."

"There's still something I don't quite understand. Earlier, you mentioned my mother died giving birth to me."

"Yes, that's correct, Miss."

"You then said after the doctor told everyone to leave the room, and my father returned just moments later; he wanted answers as to what just happened. However, you did not say that my father was still devistated that he had lost his wife?"

"No, I did not because there was no reason for him to be."

"You mean to tell me my mother's alive?" she asks, looking Ansel in the eye.

"Yes."

Chapter Four

At an undisclosed location, the Order of the Black Veil gathers in a dimly lit room. They begin an initiation ritual. A young man stands before the order wearing nothing but a blindfold around his eyes. Two order members guide him over to a concrete slab where he lays flat on his back. Thibauld and his father sit side by side, watching as the other members sink their teeth into the young man's flesh. It's not long before the ritual is over. Paulo stands up from a leaning position, with a handkerchief from his jacket pocket he wipes the young man's blood from his lips.

Paulo looks toward Thibauld and his father.

"I'm afraid I must be going now. Regrettably, I have committed myself to a separate engagement."

"No trouble at all, Paulo," Thibauld says with a nod. "We look forward to seeing you at the next one."

"I'll be there," Paulo replies as he walks towards the door and leaves the room, exiting the building Paulo walks the darkened alleyways of the quiet city. He stops suddenly.

"I was in a meeting, you know," he says out loud.

"Yes I know, why did you leave so suddenly?" Asks a female voice from an unseen corner in the shadows.

Paulo shivers, "because I felt your presence, I figured you wouldn't want an audience."

"An audience for what?"

"For when you kill me."

"Why would I want to kill you, Paulo? Perhaps it's because of what happened to your dear friend Francois?"

"Yes, I can't live with the guilt any longer. I knew he wouldn't make it, and I even told him this, but the poor old fool insisted."

Abigail's mother, Collete, steps out from the shadows. Beautiful and youthful with curly brunette hair and wearing a long black dress, she slowly approaches Paulo. She smiles from the excitement of seeing an old friend. They embrace each other with a gentle hug.

"Collete, how I've missed you all these years. It's lovely to see you again, finally."

"The feeling is mutual dear Paulo. I never did get the chance to say thank you for bringing me back that day. If it weren't for you, I would have never got to see my daughter blossom into a beautiful young woman."

"She takes after her mother in that way."

"Paulo, you always did have a way with words. I suppose if you're sure you want to do things this way."

"Yes. It has to be you, Collete."

Still embracing each other, Collete places her hand on Paulo's cheek and kisses him on the lips. She pulls away slightly as he tilts his head, exposing his neck, and bites into his skin. He doesn't put up a fight but instead embraces true death. As his life begins to fade, he whispers to Collete.

"I have always loved you, sweet Collete. I'm sorry for Francois."

Chapter Five

Cariveau resident: three days after her father's death.

A thunderous knock at the door awakens Abigail. She stands up from the daybed in the living room where she was napping. As she walks into the foyer, Ansel lets Inspector Laurent inside. Abigail is surprised to see him but finds herself immediately aroused by an almost uncontrollable sexual attraction.

"Inspector, What brings you to my humble abode at such an early hour?" Abigail asks in a flirtatious tone.

"Another body was found this morning; two puncture wounds on the neck closely resembling those found on your father's body. The victim was nearly drained of all his blood." Gabriel answers.

"And are you still suggesting its rodents, as you stated previously?" Ansel inquires.

"No. Not at all."

"Perhaps a serial murderer than?" Abigail asks.

"No, I know this is going to sound insane, but I have reason to believe these killings are being done by Vampires."

Ansel and Abigail look at each other, intrigued by Gabriel's statement.

"I think we're gonna need a spot of tea for this conversation," Ansel says while gesturing Abigail to take Gabriel to the living room.

Ansel walks into the kitchen to make the tea. When he enters the living room Abigail and Gabriel are sitting across from each other; Gabriel in a chair and Abigail on the couch. Ansel sets a tray of tea on the coffee table and sits in the chair next to Gabriel.

Everyone grabs a cup of tea, Gabriel begins to speak.

"Nearly 400 years ago, there was a man by the name of Vlad Dracul the third, born in Transylvania and later to rule over Wallachia, Romania. Some people say he was the first, but no one really knows for sure. Much more recently, there's been a rash of brutal killings all over the world. Each one of the victims drained of their blood with puncture wounds on the neck; the body tossed away like garbage. I've done some digging, and from what I can tell, it all started in Versailles several years ago. It was reported that a young girl from the village, who was about the same age you are now." Gabriel says while looking at Abigail.

She casually sips her tea, listening to every word he says.

Gabriel continues, "Some of the locals claimed they had seen the girl attack a farmer who was working the fields early that morning. A neighbor of his ran over to help, but when he got over there, the girl ran off, and a chunk of the farmer's neck had been bitten off. I believe that little girl was a vampire."

"Why are you coming to us with this? Why not take it to your colleagues?" Ansel asks.

"Do you think if I had, they would've believed me?"

"No, I suppose not."

"But that doesn't explain why you come to us with this theory." Abigail chimes in.

Gabriel stands from the couch and places his cup of tea on the table; he reaches into his pocket and removes a folded paper. It was an old newspaper report. He handed it to Abigail, who unfolds it and reads it. It wasn't long before she saw the name of the little girl was Collete.

"Collete Valiquette," Gabriel looks Abigail in the eyes. "I believe that was your mother's name, correct?"

Though she's not sure why Abigail becomes visibly upset, a tear emerges from her eye. Ansel sets his cup down and stands from his chair. Turning his attention to Gabriel, he gestures toward the foyer.

"I do believe, Sir, it's time for you to make your exit. I'll show you the door." Ansel says with disdain.

After escorting Gabriel out, Ansel returns to the living room where Abigail sits staring at the newspaper report about the young Collete. Ansel sits next to her and says nothing. She lays her head on his shoulder.

"Do you think my mother could be evil?" Abigail asks.

"Not at all, madam. The Collete I knew was always the kindest and gentlest soul I had ever had the pleasure of being around. She would always make sure everyone around her was happy, and she would always put her happiness last."

Abigail was feeling weak from being awake during the day; it was an affliction she has lived with since birth. She falls asleep with her head still on Ansel's shoulder. He doesn't want to disturb her, so he sits there next to her until she reaches deep sleep.

Chapter Six

May 11, 1792, It has been two months since the death of her father, Francois. Abigail has gotten used to her new abilities and has learned how to use them with the help of Ansel, her loyal butler. The rest of her staff has since been let go; Abigail didn't want to risk anyone else finding out about what she had become. She's been avoiding people at all costs in fear she might lose control of the gift she has been given. She had spent most of her time inside her home with the doors locked and windows closed. Anyone who came to the door would be turned away.

This was the first time Abigail has been outside in over a month. She felt the urge to walk the streets of Paris and hunt for the first time since her rebirth. Feeling an overwhelming sense of excitement, she comes up to a bar that looks like it was intentionally hidden from the public. She walks into the bar and meets the eyes of a man across the room. He looks at her and smiles, excusing himself from his group of friends he follows

Abigail as she walks back out through the door. She keeps her distance, but still, he follows as if her beauty hypnotizes him. Or maybe it was her perfume that attracted him. Whatever it was, he was mesmerized.

Abigail leads the man into a dark alley and up a narrow set of steps. She goes inside an old run-down flat and shuts the door between them. The man enters to see a living room with no furniture. Candles set atop the fireplace mantel give off just enough for him to see Abigail walk into the next room. He follows, immediately noticing the bed. Its condition was not up to most people's standards, but neither of them seems to care. Abigail approaches the man and, without saying anything, rips his shirt off; it falls to the floor. She grabs him by the neck and picks him up, throwing him onto the bed, then jumps on top of him.

"Miss, careful now. I wasn't quite expecting this." The man says.

"Shhhhh," Abigail says, placing a finger on his lips, then uses her hand to start unbuttoning her blouse a bit.

The man lays, watching and enjoying every minute.

Abigail leans forward, brushing her breast across his bare chest and whispers in his ear, "Do you like what you see?"

"Oh, yes, I do indeed." He says.

She sits back up and traces a single fingernail from his neck down his chest, causing him to quiver underneath her.

"Mmmmm, I like making you move beneath me." She says, "I wonder what else I can make you do?"

She leans in again, this time she licks from his collar bone to his neck, then bites.

"Ah! Hey, I'm not into that kind of thing."

"Quiet! Or I will do it more."

He quiets down, and then Abigail begins moving around on him more. Reaching down under her skirt, she releases his manhood, "I want information, and if you give it to me, I will give you what you desire."

"What kind of information?"

"Names, eight of them to be precise."

"Whose names?"

"The leaders of The Order of the Black Veil." She says in a sultry hiss as she begins to move her hips...although he's not inside her yet. She continues, "for every name you give me, I will slide you inside me and thrust you as deep as you can go."

"What makes you think I can get you these names?"

Abigail snarls like a rabid animal and uses her arms to pin him to the bed.

"Don't play games. I've been watching you all night. I watched you deliver eight pieces of correspondence to eight different addresses. Each envelope marked with the same seal on the back."

"If I give you those names, they'll kill me."

"You should be more concerned with what I'll do if you don't give me the names," Abigail warns.

She leans down to bite his neck again.

"No. Wait, wait, wait!" he says while flinching.

"Names. Now!" Abigail snarls again.

The man reaches down and pulls a list from his pants pocket, handing it to Abigail he smiles.

"Shall we continue, Miss?"

"No, I've gotten what I came for, so I'll be taking my leave now."

She climbs off of him and closes her blouse.

"Enjoy the rest of your evening," she says as she turns toward the bedroom door.

Abigail leaves the flat and returns home.

Chapter Seven

At the Devereux residence, Thibauld and his father Jean-Luc stand in the study having a discussion.

"Thibauld, my dear boy. The elders have been keeping a watch on you. They tell me you're causing a lot of unwanted attention as of late, and they're not very happy."

"Who cares if the elders are happy or unhappy, they are not in charge of us, father. "

"That boy is where you're wrong. The elders can make our lives a living hell if they don't like something we're doing."

"Why does it matter what they like. They're no more powerful than we are."

"It matters because if it weren't for them, you would have succumbed to true death when you were bedridden and clinging onto the little bit of life you had left when you were just a sickly child. I had to go before the elders and beg them to let me turn you."

He places his hand on his Jean-Luc's face as he steps closer to him.

"For that father, I will be eternally grateful, and when I kill the elders, we can rise to power the way it should be; father and son side by side sitting at the head of the table as the new elders."

"They would have your head for even thinking it, and mine for having heard it."

"Listen to what you just said, father. They would put us to death just because we think our own thoughts. Does that sound like a group of people worth serving?"

"Bite your tongue, boy. You never know who might be listening."

"It's who isn't listening that concerns me. You are no longer the man I knew as a child. You are nothing but a shadow of the man you once were, nothing more than a puppet with strings pulled by the elders. You are nothing at all."

"How dare you speak to me that way I am your father!!"

"My father is dead!!!" Thibauld screams as he jabs his fingers into his father's chest and removes his heart. He kicks Jean-Luc's body through the window of the study and watches as it falls to the street below.

Chapter Eight

Abigail is in a bathtub of warm water, Ansel with his back turned toward her speaks.

"Tell me, madam, what do you intend to do with this list of names you received?"

"Well, Ansel, I'm going to start at the top and work my way down. Killing these men one by one. I have reason to believe that these were the men who killed my father."

"I completely understand that, but this is all still very new to you. These men have been members of the Black Veil for years, which stands to reason they've been undead for just as long. They are much stronger than you are."

"What are you saying exactly, Ansel? Are you saying I shouldn't do this? I should just stay home and let my father's death be in vain?"

"No madam, not at all. I'm simply stating that you have to be careful. You have to be smarter than your enemy. The best way to do this is to take our time. We need to know more about them than they know about themselves."

"And how do you propose we do that?" Abigail asks.

"We watch and we wait until the opportune moment. That's when we go in for the kill. Now, who is the first name on the list?"

"Marius Babineaux."

"Okay, great tomorrow morning I'll follow his every move while you stay home and sleep. Once I get back, I'll give you every bit of information I get."

"Okay, Ansel, we can try it your way."

Early the next morning, Ansel stands at a street corner. A child comes over to him and points to a building across the street.

"He's coming out now, Sir." says the child.

"Thank you very much, young man. One livre as promised." Ansel replies while handing a coin to the child. "Now, can you tell which one he is?"

The child points to a middle-aged man; he was about five foot nine inches in height with a slender build and black hair that shone as if he had just walked through the rain.

While keeping his distance, Ansel follows Marius as he walks down the sidewalk and stops at a corner bistro. Marius sits down at one of the outside tables. A young woman brings him a cup of tea. He hadn't been there long enough to order anything. Ansel takes this to mean Marius is a regular customer that frequents this particular bistro every day. Standing at a flower shop, Ansel watches as Marius finishes his tea and stands up, leaving payment on the table.

He continues walking, Ansel closely following behind him as he turns the corner. When Ansel rounds the corner, Marius glances back as if he knew he was being watched. Ansel quickly ducks into an alley, hoping he wasn't seen and, for extra caution, decides to enter a side entrance into a bakery. After waiting for a few moments to let some time pass and ensure Marius was not still looking for him, he carefully exits the way he entered. Peering out, Ansel does not see Marius, so he resumes his walk to try to locate him again, but Marius is nowhere to be found. He decides, even though it's still early, he's going to return home and tell Abigail what he has witnessed.

"I followed him just as I said I would. I lost track of him, but he might suspect I was following him. I very much doubt he would even know who I work for even if I had gotten caught."

"Where did you say you lost track of him?" asks Abigail.

"In the alleyway behind the bistro and the bakery."

"Okay. When the sun goes down, I'll head over there and take a look around."

"As you wish, Miss."

Later that night, Abigail watches the bistro alleyway from the roof across the street. A man exits the bistro from the back door. A young woman stands by the door and collects tips as the man is leaving. Abigail sees an opportunity and takes it. She jumps down from the roof and onto a balcony where she leaps down to the street. Abigail walks across over to the bistro alley. The young woman notices her right away and is taken aback by the sight of her beauty. Abigail smiling slowly approaches the woman. A grin flashes across her face just as she lowers her head with insecurity. Abigail places two fingers under the young woman's chin and gently guides her head upwards.

"Never hide your beauty away from the world. Keep your head held high and prove to everyone, the world is yours," says Abigail as she leans in and kisses the woman on the lips.

She walks past her and enters the bistro and is shocked to see a room full of sexual torture devices and men and women acting as submissives and dominants. A nude man with his head in a stockade, being spanked by a large wooden paddle. A naked woman was tied to a St. Andrews cross. Abigail looks around and sees several other things happening all at once; she is aroused but remains focused. She walks up the stairs and on the wall at the top is a portrait of the Marquis De Sade. An older woman who looked to be about fifty years old approaches.

"Do you see anything you like?" the woman asks.

"Yes I like it all, but I'm looking for someone, can you tell me where to find Marius Babineaux? We have a play date scheduled for this evening."

"Oh, of course. You'll find him just through those doors." The woman says while stepping out of Abigail's way.

Abigail approaches the door to the room and enters. She sees Marius is entirely nude, tied to a whipping bench face down with a leather gag in his mouth and a blindfold around his eyes. A woman in a leather executioner's mask stands nearby with a nine-tailed whip in her hand. Abigail places a finger to her lips, gesturing for the woman to stay quiet. She obliges and leaves the room, passing the whip to Abigail, who is now alone with Marius. She approaches the whipping bench running her fingernails across his back.

Leaving red scratch marks, he twitches as a cold chill runs up his spine. Abigail cracks the whip across his lower back, and it leaves a few welts. Marius winces ever so slightly. Abigail smirks but keeps her silence as she circles the whipping bench. She cracks the whip again this time even harder, leaving welts on his ass. She strikes him again and again until the whip cuts into his skin and causes him to bleed ever so slightly. She is once again aroused. Marius is enjoying the abuse, she strikes again and hears him scream through the leather gag, but the sound is muffled. Abigail throws the whip on the floor and takes a thick leather strap off the wall that is hanging from a hook. The strap was long with six metal studs at the end. With a heavy swing, Abigail hits him as hard as she can. Blood drops from the tiny holes in his back, then she jumps on him and bites into his neck until her lust for blood is satisfied.

Chapter Nine

Neville Beauchamp is the next name on the list. He stands in a cemetery kneeling in front of a headstone; it reads Victoria Ann Beauchamp, born September 6th, 1789, died December 26, 1790.

"What happened to her?" Abigail asks from a few feet behind him.

"No one really knows for sure. She was a healthy child, so full of energy. She wore us out just watching her play even though she was less than a year old. She still played in our arms, squeezing our fingers and smiling. She had just started crawling; she was such a bright child." He smiles at the thought of his memory then continues, his gaze turning sorrowful. "Then, one morning, she fell ill. She felt so hot to the touch, and little bumps appeared all over her body. The doctor could not get to us in time, and she passed away a short time later." He responds.

"And the child's mother?" Abigail asks.

"Could not deal with the pain. While I was away, she hung herself from the wooden beam in the attic. All the years of us trying so hard to have a child, just for her to be taken from us so young. The stress was too much for her."

"Take a walk with me." Says Abigail. "Tell me the tragic tale of Victoria Ann Beauchamp."

The two of them begin walking through the cemetery, and Neville starts telling the story.

"I remember it like it was yesterday, February 17, 1776. I was at a gathering of politicians and their advisors and a few others. There I was, pulled into a debate between a couple of men. I have no idea what the debate was about back then, and for the life of me, I can't even figure it out now. As they stood arguing, I looked past them, and from across the room, I locked eyes with the most beautiful woman I had ever seen. She was petite with long blonde hair and ruby red lips with a smile that could light up a room. The moment I saw her, everyone else in the room faded away. I knew they were still there, but I only saw her. I've always had trouble approaching women, and even more trouble trying to hold a conversation with them; nevertheless, I approached her with ease. I was still nervous, but after a few minutes, I managed enough courage to ask her if I could court her. She agreed and soon after we fell in love, then we married a year later. It didn't take long before she started saying how she desired children. I wanted to give her everything she had ever hoped for, so we tried for several years, but alas were unsuccessful. We sought out doctors from all over, trying to find a way to have a child together. We even talked to a woman claiming to be a witch. We were desperate. Finally, after more than ten years just when we had given up the hope of having children, she became pregnant as if by some miracle from God and Victoria was born," Neville pauses.

"What was your wife's name?" Asks Abigail.

"Elizabeth, she's buried directly on the other side of Victoria," Neville replies.

"That's beautiful. A mother should be buried next to her child." Abigail says as a tear rolls down her cheek.

"And I should be buried right alongside them, that is my last request."

"So, you already know why I'm here?" She asks.

"Yes. I knew it the second I felt you standing behind me. I only ask two things."

"Tell me, and I will be sure it gets done."

"First, walk me back to my wife and child. Second, I don't want to suffer. I want it done and over with quickly, so that I may rejoin my family in the afterlife."

"I will honor both requests," Abigail says while gently taking hold of Neville's hand.

They silently walk back to his family's graves, arm in arm. Neville kneels between the two graves, Abigail still holding his hand kneels with him.

"Are you ready?"

"Yes." He replies.

He lays down on the grass. Abigail gently pulls his wrist toward her mouth and bites, sucking the blood from the wound until Neville loses consciousness and succumbs to a beautiful death.

Abigail stands to her feet and leaves the cemetery. A short time later, she returns home, where Ansel has prepared dinner.

"Dinner is ready, Miss," Ansel says as Abigail enters the house.

"I'm not very hungry right now, Ansel, but thank you."

"Beg your pardon, but you wouldn't want our guest to dine alone, would you?"

"Our guest?" she asks with an expression of confusion.

Abigail walks toward the dining room and peeks her head around the corner and is shocked to see Thibauld.

"Abigail. How lovely to see you. You look the picture of health, which is saying a lot after taking a tumble off the roof." says Thibauld as he forks a bite of food into his mouth.

Abigail fully enters the dining room and sits down directly across the table from him.

"I died because of you and your inability to keep your hands to yourself."

"That's your way of looking at it, but the way I see it, you are more alive than you've ever been all because of my inability to keep my hands to myself," Thibauld replies with a smile and a wink. He forks more food into his mouth.

"How did you know I was still alive?" Abigail asks.

"Well, that's an easy question to answer. I was at the dungeon room the night you killed my colleague, Marius. The dungeon room is what they call the bistro at night."

"So I gathered," she says. "What do you mean you were there? I don't recall seeing you at all."

"No, I suppose even with your new ability, you wouldn't have seen me either way. I was in a hidden room right next to his. I get pleasure from watching. I'm sure you must've felt my presence."

"I felt someone might be watching, but I wasn't sure who. All I know is, I was enjoying myself, so I didn't care who saw. How did you know about my new ability?" asks Abigail.

"We all get new abilities when we are reborn. When you sat down, I could see a slight glow in your eyes, which wasn't there before. This told me your new ability has something to do with sight."

"And what ability did you get when you were reborn?" she inquires.

"Because I was weak and sickly when I was born, my new ability in rebirth was strength. I'm much stronger than most of our kind. You more than likely received the gift of sight because when you were born human, you were blind to the world of the supernatural."

"I look forward to the day I get to test your ability and see how strong you really are," Abigail says with a grin.

"And you shall have that day, my dear Abigail, but today is not the day," Thibauld says as he wipes a handkerchief across his mouth and stands up from his chair. "I only dropped by to check on you and tell you to be careful. There are some dangerous creatures out there, and I'm not talking about me."

He walks past Abigail and into the foyer, where he nods at Ansel and leaves through the front door.

"What did the young man want, Miss?" Ansel asks as Abigail joins him in the foyer.

"He claims he just wanted to come by and check on me, told me there were some dangerous creatures out there and that I should be careful."

"Who or what do you think he was talking about?"

"I'm not really sure, but I'm sure we'll find out soon enough," Abigail replies.

Chapter Ten

Thibauld casually walks through the streets of Paris, whistling with a smile on his face. He winks at a beautiful woman passing by, she smiles and continues on her way. Thibauld stops in front of a workhouse and enters. He is then stopped by a big brute of a man, as he walks through the door.

"What is your business here?" he asks Thibauld.

"My business is with the man upstairs, Archibald Merryweather. Tell him my name is Thibauld Devereux and that I wish to speak to him about a private matter. He'll know who I am."

The brute walks up the stairs and into the office, seconds later, he returns.

"Mr. Merryweather will see you now, head on up."

"Thanks, big guy," Thibauld says with a smile as he walks past the brute.

He heads upstairs and enters the office where Archibald sits behind his desk. A young worker stands in the corner of the room, her clothes covered in dirt and her body covered in cuts and bruises. Thibauld looks at her for a few seconds then returns his focus to Archibald.

"What happened to her?" Thibauld asks.

"She was hired to do a job. The job was incomplete, so the client wanted her for a different task. She refused, but he took what he wanted from her anyway." Archibald replies.

"Has this happened to a lot of your workers?"

"That, Mr. Devereux, is nothing you should concern yourself with. Now, how about you tell me why you wanted this little meeting?"

"Well, I'm sure as you probably know by now, my father is dead."

"Yes, an unfortunate accident," Archibald replies with a hint of sarcasm.

"It was indeed. Anyway, his seat has been empty for a few weeks now, and I would like to fill it, I heard you were the man to ask."

"Never liked your father very much. I consider him a brother but never a friend. He was elected into that seat because he was the most deserving. You, on the other hand, do not deserve it at all. I like you even less than I liked your father. He was going to be the next in line to be chosen as an elder because he was always so loyal to the cause. The rest of the council of elders and I discussed it for a very long time. We were planning on announcing it soon, but I guess that's not going to happen now."

"Give me his seat in the order, and I swear I'll show you how deserving I am of the council position," Thibauld replies with a childlike tone of frustration.

"Understand something, young Devereux. You will never get a seat on the council. Especially since you were already drawing attention to our existence, but because we suspect you murdered your father. You wanted to get our attention, and so you have."

"Let's see if they pay attention to this," Thibauld says, picking up an iron letter opener shaped like the sword of a medieval knight. He throws it with all his strength; it pierces Archibald's heart and keeps going exiting through the skin of his back and sticking into the wall behind him. Archibald's body hits the floor; Thibauld turns his attention to the girl and slowly approaches the girl who couldn't have been a day over eighteen years old. She stands frozen with fear.

"Don't be afraid, deary. I wouldn't dare dream of harming a hair on your head, take my hand and let me help you embrace your true destiny."

The girl takes his hand, he pulls her close, and with his other hand, he tilts her head and brushes her hair back with his fingers. He gently kisses her neck before piercing her flesh with his sharp teeth. She winces in pain but leans back in pleasure.

Later that same evening in the club hidden in an alleyway away from the public. Abigail walks into the establishment. She immediately notices, standing on a small stage, is Thibauld. The room goes quiet, and everyone in the crowd locks eyes with him. Thibauld clears his throat. He begins singing.

"La reverie
Dream of me
Blood of mine
A lust divine.
Walk with me through the sands of time.
...
I will call to you
You will come to me
La reverie
Dream of me."

Thibauld sings with the voice of an angel. Abigail leans against the bar as she listens to him belt out the lyrics in their entirety. She sees a beautiful young girl standing by the stage looking at Thibauld longingly. Abigail approaches the girl.

"Hello, I'm Abigail. What's your name?"

"I am Jazmyne."

"You look like you're a little out of place. Are you sure you should be here?"

"I have nowhere else to go. Thibauld told me I should feel at home here."

"You know Thibauld?"

"Yes. " Jazmyne replies. "He saved my life this afternoon when he took me away from the workhouse."

"Abigail, are you bothering my new pet?" Thibauld says as he leaps from the stage, having finished his song. "You should be ashamed of yourself."

"No worries, Thibauld. Jazmyne and I were just getting to know each other."

"Well, isn't that delightful? "He says enthusiastically. "May I suggest we all head upstairs and truly get better acquainted with each other?"

Abigail cringed when she heard the notion, but after a few seconds, she found herself becoming aroused at the thought of Thibauld"s suggestion. The three ascend the stairs to a private room on the second floor. A young man stands guard as the three enter the room and pull the door closed behind them. Abigail doesn't waste time and immediately begins kissing Jazmyne. She caresses Jazmyne as she runs a hand up her leg and inner thigh. Thibauld joins them by approaching Jazmyne from behind. He rips her dress in the back and lets it drop to the floor. Abigail bends slightly and sinks her teeth into Jazmyne"s breast.

"You girls continue. It seems I've forgotten something."

Thibauld approaches the door to the room and opens it. He peeks his head out and with a finger gestures for the young man guarding the entrance.

The young man smiles and enters the room. After once again closing the door, Thibauld pushes the young man against the wall and tears his shirt open and bites him on his chiseled chest. The young man returns the favor and is joined by Abigail and Jazmyne. All four of them begin kissing, biting, and rubbing each other all over. Jazmyne steps between Thibauld and the young man now, rubbing her ass against Thibauld while biting the young man on the neck. While the three of them are enjoying each other, Abigail decides to kneel and lift Jazmyne's skirt so that she can get a bite of her thigh. Thibauld bites Jazmyne on her shoulder, then notices what Abigail is doing. He grabs her by the arm to make her stand, then looks into her eyes and moves toward her, gazing at her neck. Abigail steps back.

"I should go. I should have turned away the minute he suggested it." She thought to herself.

Abigail leaves the room and exits the club disappearing into the dark of the night.

Chapter Eleven

The village of Versailles. A young redhead girl walks by a stream surrounded by woods. She listens to the sounds of the whistling wind and the chirping of birds in the early evening sun. As she walks barefoot across the moist grass, she hears a humming from behind the trees.

"Hello? is anybody there?" asks the girl.

"Yes. I'm here." says a handsome young man as he steps out from the trees.

The man is tall with medium length hair as black as the night sky.

"You seem to be overdressed for a stroll through the forest, Sir," she remarks with a smile as she observes his waistcoat.

"You have nothing to protect your feet, Miss. It seems we're both a little out of our element," he replies with a charming grin.

"Where are you from? I don't recall seeing you around here before," she says.

"No, I suspect you wouldn't have. I've only just arrived a couple of days ago. This is my first time actually getting the chance to explore this little village of yours."

"And how are you liking it so far?" she asks.

"It's almost as beautiful as you are."

" Are you here for long?" she asks, still smiling about his compliment.

"Regrettably no. I must be moving on in the next few days."

"Where are you staying?"

"The château just up the hill. It's quite a lovely place, have you seen it?" He asks.

"Yes but I've never been inside this is also the first chance I've had to explore

I've only just moved here a short time ago."

"Come with me, and I'll show you around."

Usually, she would never go off to a strange place with a man she's never met before, but for some reason, she found the man to be irresistible and agreed to accompany him back to the château. A short walk from the stream in the woods and they arrive. The château is beautiful from the outside, but when she enters the inside, she immediately falls in love with the place. White candles line the walls in the corridor and on the staircase. Black curtains hang in front of the windows, and a red rug lies on the floor between the stairs and the front door.

He takes her by the hand and leads her up the stairs and into the bedroom, neither of them speaking a single word. He kisses her passionately as he lays her gently on the bed.

"Dance with me," he says, whispering into her ear.

They make love. When the redhead girl wakes up the next morning, the man is gone.

Abigail wakes up, confused about the dream she just had; questions plagued her mind. "Who was that man? Was the woman my grandmother? What was the meaning behind such a dream." She hears a knock on the door downstairs and rushes out of her room and down the staircase. Ansel opens the door; both of them are surprised to see Inspector Gabriel Laurent.

"Gabriel, what are you doing here?" Abigail asks from the bottom of the stairs.

"Well, I thought I would come by and tell you the body count is getting higher and higher. First, your father's body was found covered in bite marks. Then Paulo, who was his best friend, was found dead in a dark alleyway. Mr. Devereux goes missing, Marius Babineaux was found floating in the river beaten and bitten. Neville Beauchamp is found in the cemetery with his blood drained, and now Archibald Merryweather is found dead in his office, his body on the floor with his heart stuck to the wall with a letter opener."

"Why are you telling me all this?" Abigail asks.

"I'm telling you this because I think I'm in over my head. I know Paris has a serious vampire problem, and I also know that people who are bitten become vampires only if they are born with the genetics. Last time I was here I noticed the puncture marks on your neck, every other time I have seen those marks, the person has been dead. That tells me that you, Abigail, are a vampire."

"What's the next step, inspector?" Asks Abigail. "Are you going to kill me? Or Arrest me for murders I didn't commit?"

"You're the least of my worries," he sighs. "I was hoping I could count on your help to bring down the order of the black veil."

"Only if you promise to tell nobody else what I am," she replies with a warning.

"I give you my word if you help me; your secret will never pass through these lips."

"Let's talk in here," says Abigail as she gestures toward the living room.

"I'll put the tea on." Says Ansel closing the front door.

In the living room, Abigail and Gabriel sit down across from one another. She pulls the list of names from her cleavage and marks Paulo and Archibald off.

"What's that?" Gabriel asks.

"This is a list of eight names. Each man is a leader in the order. Archibald and Paulo are now off the list." Abigail hands him the list.

"There are only three names left, did you kill the other five?"

"No," she says I only killed Neville Beauchamp and Marius Babineaux. Well, it looks like someone is helping you...

Chapter Twelve

Thibauld stands before the council of elders, their faces cloaked, and one of their voices at a whispered tone; the second said nothing at all.

"Thibauld, would you care to explain why we are the only two elders left on this council when there should be six of us?"

"Something tells me you already know the answer to that question. Something tells me that no matter what I have to say, it won't make a difference, and it won't change what happens here tonight."

"Be that as it may. We want to hear an explanation."

"Okay, have it your way. As I'm sure you know already, my father, in the hopes of gaining a seat of power on the council of elders, was just the first step. The second step was trying to talk me into the position. So I paid a visit to your good friend Archibald, the discussion started out friendly enough with an exchange of what he would describe as pleasantries. Things got heated when we spoke of my father, and he insulted me; for that reason, among other things, I felt I was left with no other choice but to kill him."

"And what about the others that were killed? Did you decide that two murders were not enough, and you wanted to bring more attention to yourself and to our existence?"

"I assure you those other three murders were not my doing. I was shocked to find out about Paulo and Neville. Not really surprised about Marius."

The elders turn to look at each other surprised to hear Thibauld didn't kill the others.

"Tell us. If not you, then who was it that killed these men?"

At the Cariveau home. A heavy pounding on the front door. Ansel opens it to a shirtless bloody and beaten Thibauld. He passes out and falls to the floor between the steps and the foyer. Abigail and Gabriel help Ansel drag him inside. Ansel pushes the door closed, then the three of them carry Thibauld to the sofa in the living room and lay him down with his head propped up. Ansel rushes out of the room and returns with a towel and a bowl of water to clean Thibauld's wounds.

"What happened to you?" Ansel asks while wiping some blood from Thibauld's face.

"Who cares?" Abigail interrupts. "Whatever happened to him, I'm certain he probably deserved it."

"That's where you're wrong, dearest, Abigail." Thibauld replies in a weakened voice. "this time, I was trying to do the right thing."

Abigail kneels down closer to him.

"What do you mean by that?" She asks.

"I went to see the council of elders," Thibauld says, leaning up ever so slightly and wincing in pain. I was hoping to get appointed into a position of power, so I could keep an eye on them, and try to figure out precisely what it is they have planned. I guess they didn't like what I was doing, they never have."

"What exactly were you doing, Mr. Devereux?" Asks Gabriel. "And who are these elders that you speak of?"

"Quiet let him tell his story," says Abigail in a demanding tone.

"The council felt I was drawing too much attention to myself." Thibauld continues. "They found out that I have been hunting down council members one by one and thought I should be punished for my actions."

"What did they do to you?" Asks Ansel still cleaning Thibauld's wounds.

"After shackling my arms and legs to the wall of the council chambers, they cut the shirt off of my back and began beating me. They wouldn't stop, and it felt like it went on forever.

Abigail visualizes Thibauld's ordeal in her head. She could see the excruciating pain that he had to endure. And just when the beating stopped, Thibauld got 60 lashes from a leather whip with an iron tip on the tail.

"I don't even remember how I got here," Thibauld says. "Last thing I remember is waking up to the sight of you standing over me."

"Never mind all that," Gabriel interjects. "I just heard you confess to multiple murders give me one good reason why I shouldn't arrest you and have you put to death."

"How about two good reasons?" Thibauld replies. "Reason one is you probably have no idea how to kill me."

"And reason number two," Abigail says, interrupting. "We Vampires aren't subject to human laws. We handle things our own way."

"Took the words right out of my mouth," Thibauld says with a grin and a look of confusion.

Gabriel sits down and says nothing. He knew they were right and accepted the fact that no vampire would ever see the inside of a jail cell unless they wanted to be there. Abigail and Thibauld continue talking while Ansel leaves the room with the bowl of water and now bloody towel in his hand.

"Earlier, you mentioned that the council of elders has something their planning," says Abigail. "Do you know what they have in mind?"

"I'm not sure of when they're planning it, but I know what they want to do." Thibauld replies. "The head of the council wants to cleanse the world of the human race. A vampire revolution where only a few humans are left alive to feed off of when necessary."

"How are they going to do it?" Gabriel chimes in.

"Not sure, but I might know where they can be found if you move fast enough."

"Let's go," Gabriel says as he stands from the chair.

"Gabriel, no. I'll handle this. You go home." Abigail says in a demanding tone once again.

He does as she says and leaves the living room, then exits the Cariveau home. Gabriel decides to take a walk and clear his head. He walks a few blocks before realizing how late it is and noticing he is the only one still out and about. He thinks nothing of it and continues on his way a few more blocks. Gabriel stops suddenly and hears the faint sound of a woman crying coming from an alleyway nearby. He races in the direction he believes it to be coming from. The cry grows louder and louder every few feet. Finally, he sees her, the beautiful eternally youthful Collete. Having never met her before, he didn't know Abigail's supposedly deceased mother was the woman who stood before him.

"Madam? Is everything okay?" Gabriel asks as he slowly steps closer.

"I'm fine now. Sadly the same can not be said for you." Collete replies.

She lunges toward him, he lets out a blood-curdling scream, but his screams go unheard in the quiet of the night air as she bites into his neck ripping at his flesh with her teeth until he falls to the ground to meet his untimely death.

Chapter Thirteen

Abigail arrives at the warehouse, where the council of elders had set up their headquarters. She wasn't shocked to see that everything had been cleared out. Other than a few drops of Thibauld's blood on the floor, it looked as though the building had been out of use for years. Abigail knew that if The Order of The Black Veil went into hiding, it would be a long time before she could track them down. Abigail knew she needed to get back to the house to take care of Thibauld. If there were going to be a vampire revolution, she would need all the help she could get to stop it. Leaving the old warehouse, Abigail starts walking back to her house, which was about a mile away. With every step she took, she could feel a presence watching her. Abigail stays cautious and prepares herself for an attack but it never comes.

She is now three blocks away from her humble abode when an overwhelming feeling of sorrow came over her. She uses her ability and peers through the dark of an alleyway to see a body on the ground. As she gets closer, she realizes its Gabriel, the inspector.

"Who did this to you, Gabriel?" she asks while kneeling next to his lifeless body.

"It was the most brutal thing I've ever witnessed." A voice says from the shadows as Jazmyne steps into the light. "I watched as his throat was torn out."

Jazmyne, what are you doing out here? Paris isn't safe after sundown come with me, let's get you inside." Abigail says with concern in her voice.

Jazmyne does as Abigail asks and follows her back to the Cariveau home. Upon entering the home, Abigail turns to Jazmyne.

"Why were you out there alone?" you should be more careful at least until you know more about the evils of the world."

"I know, but Thibauld asked me to keep an eye on anyone coming to this house or leaving from it," Jazmyne replies.

"Why would he ask you to keep an eye on the company I keep?"

"Because he is in love with you." says a young man with short blonde hair and a body so muscular, he could've been the model for the statue of David.

"Who are you and why are you in my house?" Abigail asks with an angry tone.

"His name is Artemis; you've met before." Jazmyne interrupts. "He was in the room with us," she says.

Abigail now recognizes the young man as the one guarding the door on the night that she first met Jazmyne.

"That doesn't answer the question of why you're here in my home."

"Jazmyne came to get me when she found out Thibauld had been hurt. She mentioned something about you leading us into battle against the Order of the Black Veil."

"I never said anything about leading anyone into battle," Abigail says, looking at Jazmyne. "And if you were outside the whole time, how did you know about the vampire revolution?"

"It's my gift, heightened hearing from long distances away. The furthest away I've been so far is the alley across the street." Jazmyne says pridefully.

"What gift do you have?" Abigail asks, turning her attention to Artemis.

"I have the inexhaustible agility. If you had continued playing with us the other day, you would already know that." Artemis replies with the wink of an eye.

"Well, never mind that now," Abigail says. "I'm no leader, and there's no way we can go to war with the order; there's only three of us."

"Maybe you better count again, dearest Abigail," Thibauld says, appearing in the doorway.

Jazmyne smiles and runs to embrace him; he winces in pain as she throws her arms around him.

"Thanks for the offer Thibauld, but clearly, you're in no condition for a fight," Abigail replies.

"None of you are ready." Ansel chimes in holding a tray with five cups of tea. "Your training starts at sundown tomorrow evening, and I'll have no arguments about it."

The next evening, Ansel keeps to his word and begins training the four young vampires how to engage in combat.

"Far as I can tell, each vampire is gifted with one unique ability. Your training will be catered to help you enhance your ability, but also will help us figure out your weaknesses and how to strengthen them."

Chapter Fourteen

January 5th, 1792

It has been several months since anyone in Paris has heard from or seen the Order of the Black Veil. Thibauld, Jazmyne, and Artemis were now living with Abigail. Her home had become a kind of *safe haven* for young vampires with nowhere else to go, and Abigail would never turn her back on someone in need, Vampire or otherwise.

After training was complete, the four vampires had built themselves a small army and trained them to fight, out of 15 young vampires, only six were willing to fight, and the rest were too terrified. They were afraid the Order would come after them and get rid of their mistakes, their victims who survived.

Across town in an undisclosed location. An older man with short white hair and a thin mustache stands before the two hooded council members.

"What brings you before the council today, Cecil?" asks one of the council members in a whispered tone. The other stays silent still.

"I want out, Every high ranking official in the order is dying off one by one, and I have no desire to be the next one crossed off of someone's kill list," Cecil says with a slight tremble in his voice.

"Calm yourself, Cecil, there is no cause for panic." says the silent council member. "I can feel your heart racing. I feel that you are scared, but I assure you there's nothing to fear." She says as she removes the hood from her head.

Collete stands from her seat and approaches Cecil. Her soft voice helps to calm his nerves as she places a hand on his shoulder. He drops to his knees and bows his head.

"Cecil, you have always been the most loyal member of the order. Loyal to me and loyal to my cause. For that, I thank you, but I'm disappointed in you. You know that the penalty for leaving the order is immediate true death. Are you sure this is what you want to do?" Collete asks.

"I'm going to meet my true death, no matter what. I've made my decision, and I know the consequence, At least this way I have some say-so of when I get to die." Cecil replies.

Collete leans down and kisses the top of his head.

"You have been so good to me, Cecil. It is time for me to return the favor, do you have any final request?" She asks while taking a sword from the wall behind her.

"Yes," he replies. "Please make sure my family is well taken care of."

"Your request will be honored. Goodbye, Cecil." She says as she raises the sword and swiftly brings it down, the blade slices into the back of his neck and severs his head.

Chapter Fifteen

Abigail stands at the center of Place De La Concorde, watching from the crowd as the beheading of several citizens is taking place. She can feel the sense she's being watched and notices a handsome man staring at her from across the way. He seems familiar. Abigail approaches him, but he turns and takes his leave. She feels drawn toward him, so she follows closely, keeping him in sight and longing for him. She reaches out, but with every step, he remains out of reach. Abigail walks faster but still can not catch up to the handsome man's slow stride. Suddenly a bright red envelope falls out of his coat pocket. Abigail picks it up off the ground and calls to the man, but her voice goes unheard. He continues walking; she soon loses sight of him and stops her pursuit. As she stands on the empty sidewalk, she opens the envelope, inside is a formal invitation.

You are hereby cordially invited to

Hotel De Salm

on

October the 16th, 1793

For a Masquerade Ball

Abigail awakens in her bed. Still, dazed from the dream she just had and confused as to why the handsome man seems so familiar? Could it be the same man from her dream of Pearlina? Abigail is startled by a knock at her bedroom door.

"You may enter." She calls out while sitting up in her bed.

"Good afternoon, my dear," Ansel says as he pushes the door open and enters her room. "How are you feeling, Miss?" Ansel asks.

"I feel fine. Why do you ask?"

"Miss, you've been asleep for several months. I heard you yelling and moving around, so I came up to check on you." Ansel replies.

"What day is it?" Asks Abigail, "How much did I miss?"

"It's September the 9th." Ansel answers. "Why don't you come down for a spot of tea, and we'll have Thibauld explain everything."

"Okay. I'll be down momentarily." She replies. "What's that?" she asks, noticing a bright red envelope in his hand."

"Ah, yes, I almost forgot. Here you are, Miss, this was left on the steps outside and has your name on the front," he says, handing Abigail the envelope.

Ansel leaves the room and closes the door behind him. Abigail sits on the bed and opens the envelope. Just like in her dream, she pulls out an invitation to a masquerade ball.

"Who dropped this off, I wonder." she thought to herself while getting out of bed.

A few minutes later, she descends the staircase and walks through the foyer and into the living room. Jazmyne and Artemis are on the couch. Jazmyne sits in his lap as he wraps his arms around her waist in a loving embrace. Thibauld stands by the fireplace gazing into the flame while the fifteen younger vampires stand around nearby. Ansel pours a cup of tea for Abigail.

"So, what did I miss?" Abigail asks as she takes her cup from Ansel. "And can someone please explain to me why I slept for so long?"

"I can explain everything." says Thibauld turning to look at her." During the transition stages from human to vampire, the human part of you burns a lot of energy while trying to get used to your new-found abilities. It happened to me when I was first turned, and now it has happened to you just like it will soon happen to them." Thibauld says while gesturing toward the fifteen younglings.

"Okay, that explains that," says Abigail putting her cup to her lips and taking a sip. "So, what has the order been up to during my hibernation period?"

"Things have gotten bad," Jazmyne chimes in. Thibauld won't let the young ones go outside at all, but he won't tell anyone why."

"It's for your own protection," Thibauld rebuttals. "Everyone gathers around and listen. Now that Abigail is awake, I will explain everything to everyone."

The fifteen younglings gather in front of Thibauld and sit on the floor; everyone in the room listens intently as he begins his explanation.

"Paris France as we know it is a powder keg. The order has lit the spark, and soon, everything will go up in flames. Make no mistake; each one of us is in danger. Innocent civilians are being slaughtered and beheaded in grand fashion at Place De Concorde and put on display for all to see. Louis and the rest of the royals have turned a blind eye. They know people are being killed and no one is doing a damn thing to stop it. Humans are being killed for being human and vampires are being killed if the order views them as a potential threat. The vampire revolution has already begun, and unless we stop it, there will be no one left to feed on, and Paris, along with the rest of the world, will belong to Collete."

"My Mother?" Abigail asks angrily, "You knew this entire time that my mother was the leader of the order, and you said nothing."

"It wasn't the right time." Thibauld replies.

"And you think now was the appropriate time to bring it up," she says, still angry.

"There's probably not an appropriate time to tell a girl that her mother is an evil vampire who is hellbent on wiping out the human race. But now that you know I have to ask, will you stand with us and fight?"

"We will." Says a voice from the crowd of younglings.

Abigail looks and sees them begin to stand one by one to their feet, and one after another they speak.

"I will fight."

"I'll fight."

"I will fight with you."

"I will fight too."

The rest of them stand, "We'll fight, and we'll die for you."

At this moment, Abigail realizes the younglings look up to her. They look to her for guidance like children would look to their mother.

Ansel clears his throat, "seems to me, Miss, you've got yourself an army."

Chapter Sixteen

In the village of Versailles, in her large château, Collete sits in a relaxed position on a red chaise lounge chair in front of a roaring fireplace, basking in the warmth like a moth to the flame. Surrounded by the dark ebony wood from floor to ceiling and red velvet curtains draped across each window, she always preferred the darkness since her re-birth. She twirls her glass flute of red wine and takes a sip, licking the wine remnants from her bottom lip she begins to speak.

"For many years, I had to go into hiding. My beloved husband, Francois, thought it best to stay out of Paris. He was afraid that I might be exposed as a child of the night and hunted until my death. I did as he requested and stayed here at the château that once belonging to my grandmother Pearlina." Collete says as she looks up at a portrait of Agatha.

Collete's daughter Abigail is the spitting image of Agatha. Collete can't help but notice the similarities between the two of them. She takes another sip of wine.

"Tell me more of the beautiful Agatha." Says a male voice from across the room.

"Agatha..." Collete raises her head in acknowledgment, "Yes...dearest mother," then she gazes at the portrait even more intensely, "My grandmother, Pearlina, died giving birth to my mother, leaving her alone in this world."

"What about Agatha's father? Where was he?"

"Pearlina only saw him the one time that it took for her to get pregnant, so he never even knew he had a daughter."

"Oh, I see. Then what happened to Agatha? Who took care of her and raised her?"

"Pearlina's father gave Agatha to a servant to raise. He was ashamed that his daughter would get pregnant and not be married first. Agatha was always taught to obey no matter what the request; how to serve, and obey masters. She was never to speak unless spoken to. Never to enter a room that was occupied unless summoned first. When she disobeyed, she was beaten with a riding crop that was taken from the stables. Her beatings were so severe at times that she would bleed for hours. Not enough to kill her, but enough to make her pass out. When she was older, the masters of the house would take advantage of this, and one day, she became pregnant with me. She was forced to abandon me at an orphanage or be hung from the rafters."

"That is a very tragic life that she had to bear."

"Yes."

"And what about you, Collete? What about your childhood?"

"Mine? Well, now that is a question, isn't it? I don't remember much from my childhood before the age of seven. It wasn't until that age that I was adopted by a wealthy family. They made sure that I had all the proper schooling that a female should have; obedience, manners, music, art, but never reading or writing because a female should never have the ability to out-think a man." Collete laughs, "Such primitive thinking." she comments, then continues. "They did not know that behind closed doors, I was teaching myself. I had been sneaking into our family library and *borrowing* books, reading them at night, and hiding them under my bed. Once finished with those books, I would put them back and grab more; that's how I found out my adoptive father had formed his own secret society, which we now know as the Order of the Black Veil.

Women and children were not permitted to join the order, nor were they permitted to even be in the room while their meetings took place. Naturally, I didn't let that stop me. I always let my curiosity get the best of me as a child."

"Of course you did," says the young man across the room.

"One night before one of their meetings, I snuck into the room and hid in a small cabinet, the meeting started a few minutes later." Collete reminisces, "I left the cabinet door open ever so slightly, so I could see what was going on.

Most of the men took their seats, while four of them were called to the center of the room. The four men stood with their backs to each other. One faced north, and the other three faced south, east, and west. They began chanting together as part of a ritual, and there was a low hum coming from the rest of the room."

*"We offer this blood as a
symbol of our loyalty to our
brothers and The Order of the
Black Veil."*

"At that moment, they all sliced their forearms with the knives they were each holding in their right hands. Below on the floor in front of them were bowls that collected the blood as it dripped from their wounds." She pauses for a moment and twirls her wine glass again. "As a child, that should have scared me, but instead, I was intrigued...drawn to it, you could say. So much so that I didn't realize I had begun to lean forward. The door on the cabinet creaked, gaining my adoptive father's attention. He grabbed me by the arm and yanked me to the center of the room. Then he picked up one of the bowls, held my face so hard in his left hand; it felt like he was going to rip my jaw off. Then he poured the contents down my throat. I wrenched forward, but I did not throw it up. Instead, I stood tall and stared him down. That made him even angrier, so he grabbed me by the arm again, pulled me out of the room, and into the hallway. My adoptive mother was standing just outside the door. All he had to do was give her a look, and she turned to me and backhanded me across the face for intruding on his business. She struck me so hard it caused me to fall down the stairs." Collete sips her wine again, then continues her story.

"Since I was unconscious, it wasn't until later that I found out what happened next. Our housemaid Sylvia filled me in. She said she heard the impact of me hitting the floor at the bottom of the stairs. My adoptive parents left me lying there, So Sylvia rushed to my side and yelled for the other servants to retrieve the nearby doctor. A handsome young man named Paulo showed up, and with the help of Sylvia, I was carried outside and placed in his carriage. Sylvia insisted on riding along with us."

"What happened next?" Asks the male voice across the room.

"She said she wouldn't have believed it if she didn't see it with her own two eyes. Paulo muttered to himself that he wouldn't normally do this to a child, but there was something about me. She said he made me drink his blood, and then I woke in less than a minute. All of my wounds healed instantly as if nothing had ever happened. Paulo looked so relieved, and at the time, I didn't know why, but the look in his eyes, I will never forget. Then he turned to Sylvia, and the look he gave her even frightened me. She begged him not to hurt her and promised she would never say anything to anyone. He looked toward me as if to ask my permission to let her live to which I gave an approving nod, and then he let her out of the carriage. I never saw her again after that. I later found out from Paulo that he was hesitant at first because since I wasn't dead and because I was a child, he didn't know what the effects would be on me. He felt responsible for me now and swore an oath to me that he would never let anything bad happen to me again. He then instructed the driver to take us back to his home and told me he could not allow me to go back to those cruel people. He raised me from that point until my adulthood. The day after that incident, he somehow managed to convince my adoptive father to let him join The Order of the Black Veil. He wanted to join, so he could gather information about them and work his way up the ranks. He also said that my adoptive parents never mentioned that I was missing; they never brought my name up to anyone."

"Figures." says the male, now standing just behind Collete, placing a hand on her shoulder. "Tell me more Collete."

She takes another sip of wine and gazes back up to the portrait. "Many years went by, and every time Paulo came home, he would tell me about the meetings of the Order and updated me on the latest dealings of my adoptive parents. Now that I was an adult, I knew it was time."

"Time for what?" the male asks.

"Shh, let me tell my story."

He smirks at her comment, "Okay."

"One night, when Paulo was leaving for another Order meeting, I stopped him and told him I was coming with. He didn't question me; he only smiled. When we entered the house, I made my way to the kitchen. It was quiet since it was past dinner time and the servants had already cleaned up for the night. I grabbed a knife and then made my way to the library, where I knew my adoptive mother would be. She liked to read at night after dinner, and while her husband was holding meetings.

It kept her preoccupied. I entered the room quietly as not to disturb her or gain her attention. Her back was to me because she was sitting in a chair, much like the one I am sitting in now." Collete swirls her glass again, then continues, "I approached her and put the knife to her throat. I instructed her to stand and she did. I then made her walk, and we made our way to the meeting. She opened the door when I told her to, and we walked in. All eyes turned our direction and everyone stood as if they thought they could stop me. As soon as Paulo saw us, he seized my father and I demanded that everyone else sit. They did as I said and then I moved to the center of the room with my mother. It was set up with a table in the center this time; it was a sacrificial night. Most sacrifices were volunteers, but sometimes their sacrifices struggled, so there were straps attached to the table to hold their victims down. That night my mother was going to be the sacrifice. I told her to climb up on the table. She protested at first, but I sliced just a little into her neck, and she immediately obeyed. Once she was positioned, I secured the straps. My father tried to get out of Paulo's hold, but Paulo was much stronger than he was. I remember smiling at that. Then, I placed the bowls appropriately...one under each ankle and each wrist, slicing her as I went. She screamed in pain while everyone watched. Then I made my way back to the head of the table, and I stared every member of the Order down as I spoke,

'You all watched my adoptive father pour blood down my throat as a child, yet I did not falter. You

stood in the doorway and watched as my adoptive
mother hit me and I fell down the stairs. Yet here I
stand before you. I am Alive...I am Strong...and I
am Powerful. I am now the leader of this Order,
and if any of you defy me, you will die.'

I then sliced her throat and held another bowl filling it with her blood as my adoptive father yelled out in protest. I looked at Paulo, and he brought my father forward. I poured each of the bowls into a large one and then drowned him in my mother's blood as Paulo held him in place. Once he was dead, I turned my attention back to the members and asked,

Will any of you defy me?"

"What happened then?" the male asked.

"Well, there was silence, of course." she smiled and took another sip of her wine.

"Of course." the male says. "And what of Francois? How did you meet?"

"I had woken early that morning. Paulo entered the room and handed me a bouquet of red and white roses. He wished me a happy twenty-first birthday and requested I get dressed. A short time later, the two of us headed out the door and walked to the center of town. There was a street festival, and Paulo wanted to take me shopping. I stopped at one of the vendors, drawn to a beautiful painting of the Countess Elizabeth bathing in a tub of her victims' blood."

"I'm intrigued by a woman who has such admiration for the darkness of the world." said a voice from out of nowhere.

"I looked to see a short, stocky man standing next to me. Though he was the same height as me and slightly overweight, I was taken aback by his charm and his confidence." Collete says before continuing her story.

"My name is Francois Cariveau, and I was just on the other side of the market when I saw you, and I knew with a woman of such beauty, I had to move fast."

"Are you trying to seduce me, Mr. Cariveau?"

"Oh..ah...miss...I..ah…"

"Calm yourself, Sir. I was intrigued by your confidence and charm. Do not fail me now."

I smiled at him, and he immediately relaxed and returned the smile.

"Well, would it be too forward of me to call on you for dinner this evening?"

Just at that moment, Paulo had overheard our conversation and interjected.

"Miss, I don't think it wise to meet with strangers."

I turned to him and gave him a disapproving look, and he immediately backed down.

"Of course he did," says the mystery man, still standing behind her with his hand on her shoulder listening intently.

"I then turned to Francois and accepted his invitation. He sent a carriage for me that evening, and we dined at Chez L'Amour. It was so beautiful, decorated in my favorite colours of blood-red and black. He had told me he wanted the night to be memorable, so he chose a place he knew in his heart that I would like. We had a wonderful meal and a long conversation over the candlelit dinner. At the end of it all, we felt like we had known each other for a lifetime. He took me home and walked me to my door, putting my safety first, and making sure to show he was a gentleman. I kissed him on the cheek goodnight, and to my surprise, I found the painting of Countess Elizabeth bathing in a tub of her victims' blood in my living room waiting for me. From that moment, I knew we would be together. It was only a few months later that he asked me to marry him and I said yes. Our love was like no other. We worshiped each other, respected one another, supported each other in every way. My only regret was lying to him. I told him my adoptive parents had died in an accident, he didn't know I killed them, and he had no idea I had anything to do with the Order."

"Then how did he end up at one of the rituals? How did he even know about them?" the man asks.

"Paulo. I had died giving birth to my daughter. Francois called Paulo, knowing that he was a doctor. When Paulo arrived, he had no choice but to turn me in order to save me. He removed our family necklace, biting my neck in the process to begin my rebirth. Then he explained everything to my husband and suggested that I go into hiding. Later, Paulo told Francois that I had been captured and killed. That was right around Abigail's eighteenth birthday. Francois thought Abigail would be in danger, that the people who 'killed' me, would now come for her. Paulo took advantage of this and introduced him to one of the Order members, Jean Devereux. Jean Devereux had become Paulo's right-hand man after I took control of the Order. Meetings could no longer be held in my adoptive parent's home, so we instructed Jean Devereux to hold the meetings in his home. Paulo was jealous of our marriage and relationship. He had fallen in love with me, so he had told Jean that Francois had done something to anger me, something unforgivable and that as a punishment, I had requested the Order to perform the blood ritual on Francois, but they were to tell him the ritual was to accept him as a new member. None of the members, including Jean, questioned Paulo or brought this to my attention because they knew Paulo was my right-hand, and any instructions he gave would be the same as if I had given them myself. Ever since I had become leader, no one dared to question my orders in fear they may lose their life. So, the blood ritual happened and my sweet Francois was with me no more. Paulo knew that act would be an unforgivable one in my eyes, but he felt that if he couldn't have me, neither could Francois...both of them must die. After the ritual, I found Paulo and took his life. If I were honest with myself, I would say that I lost two loves that day. Now...now I only have the Order..." Collete places her hand on the hand still resting on her shoulder, "and you, Jacque."

Chapter Seventeen

Abigail and Thibauld are still in the living room facing each other. They continue their conversation while everyone looks on.

"What has the order been up to these last few months? And has anyone seen or heard from Collete?" Asks Abigail.

"Collete has been in hiding for some time now. As far as the Order is concerned, no one has seen or heard anything. We have no idea what their next move is. Except, I did hear that one of their top men was murdered and not by you or I. It seemed to spook a lot of them. Of course, we just added to their fear by crossing other names off the list of eight." Thibauld says with a look of concern and satisfaction. "No matter how many names have been crossed off, somehow more and more vampires are being created, and no one knows who is doing it."

"There's one thing I still don't understand," Abigail interjects. "If my mother and the Order feed off the blood of humans, Why would she want to wipe them out?"

"Collete believes we vampires are the superior race. I, for one, would have to agree, but she believes the world belongs to us. She believes a world with humans is a world prone to infections, afflictions, disease, and death."

"Well, I guess I can't argue with that," Abigail concedes. "But, the problem is, even though it would get rid of all the disease and death, it would also get rid of our food supply, and eventually we all die too. I just can't allow that."

"Well, I do know that she plans to keep some humans for herself, so she can survive. She will make sure their existence continues, but only for her benefit." Thibauld admits.

Abigail becomes very agitated, "I would really like to know what happened to her to make her such an evil woman. Nevertheless, we need a plan."

"Okay. So what *is* the plan?" asks Artemis

"War," Ansel says from the doorway as he's bringing in more tea for everyone. He sets down the tray and addresses the group. "If you will all just follow me." He turns to leave the room, and the group trails closely behind him. When they reach his bedroom door, Abigail looks confused until the door is opened to reveal the entire place filled with weapons. Weapons made to kill vampires.

"Holy hell!" Artemis exclaims.

"Um, Ansel? Where did you get all of this?" Thibauld asks as they all look upon the stash of crossbows, arrows, and spears all with iron tips. Along with stakes and crosses.

Ansel picks up a long staffed battleax with a blade on each end; the blades are pointed in opposite directions. He hands it to Abigail.

"This has been in my family for generations." He says.

Abigail flips it in her hands, "beautiful piece...which is why we are not going to use this one. Ansel, I think you need to explain yourself."

"My family is originally from Leiden Holland, and I am the nephew of Gerard Van Swieten." Ansel begins.

"I think I've heard of him, wasn't he the personal physician and advisor to the Holy Roman Empress Maria Theresa?" Jazmyne interjects, and everyone turns to her in surprise. "What? I know stuff." She says in a huff.

Ansel continues, "Yes, that is correct, Jazmyne, and it was Maria Theresa, who instructed my uncle to investigate the situations relating to vampires after the war of the Turks in 1755. As his assistant, I was brought along and in preparation for his research, he safeguarded himself and his colleagues with these weapons you see before you. After thirteen years of research, he finally submitted a report to her, indicating that the rumors were false, and there were logical explanations for the unusual states of that graves. He claimed it was from fermentation and lack of oxygen, preventing their decomposition. The result of that report made Maria Theresa issued a decree that all traditional weapons against vampires be burned. When I found this out, I snuck into my uncle's headquarters and stole them away before he had the chance to follow through on her orders. Although he didn't believe in vampires, I knew better."

"So you stole these weapons to for what reason? Because it sounds as though you had planned to use them before now." Artemis questions with confusion.

"Please don't misunderstand my intentions. I did not steal these weapons to hunt vampires. On the contrary, I kept them hidden because I knew they would be useful one day."

Everyone still looks confused.

"Allow me to explain further. As a child growing up, there were many stories of the Red Death and thieves in the night, monsters that would steal children while they sleep. Then one night, as a young gentleman in my early twenties, a monster came for me. Except, she wasn't a monster at all. She had been watching me when I was on inquiries with my uncle. She told me that she sensed I was different from my uncle. She could tell that I had a kind and compassionate heart; she was drawn to me. She warned me that if my uncle got to close to finding the truth, it would spark a war. It was her idea for me to convince him vampires weren't real. It was she who told me to steal these weapons because one day, there would be a reason to use them. She didn't give me specific details. She only told me that one day soon, there would be a war amongst the vampires, and if it weren't stopped, it would end the world as we know it. She was kind to me, and she never tried to harm me. There was something about her that connected us and told me to trust her. So I followed her instruction, and here we stand today."

"Who was she? Where is she now?" Abigail asks.

"I don't know. I never saw her again after that night." Ansel admits.

"So, we have the weapons, now we just need to figure out when and where and how," says Thibauld.

"Well, I think I know the when and the where, all we need to figure out is the how," Abigail says.

"Okay, do you mind sharing with the rest of us before we plan 'the how'? When and where exactly?" Thibauld asks.

Everyone turns to her in anticipation.

"October the 16th at Hotel De Salm, there is a masquerade ball I've been invited too," Abigail announces.

"That's perfect. Collete would never pass up a chance to be hidden in plain sight," Thibauld states.

Chapter Eighteen

Jazmyne, Artemis, and the other young vampires are loading up with weapons and preparing for war. Abigail and Thibauld leave the room to talk in private.

"So you never did tell me," Abigail says.

"Tell you what, dear Abigail?"

"When we were children, we would play together all the time, then you got sick, and your father sent you away. I didn't know until the next day and was utterly heartbroken when I heard that you were gone. I had lost my best friend and heard rumors of how you died. As a child, I believed every word of it, and after a year or so without hearing from you, I took it as confirmation that you met your death. Where were you for all those years?"

"All over the world. First Rome, that was where my father sent me to find a cure for my ailment known as Variola. He had heard tales of an apothecary from that region. It was believed that this apothecary mixed and sold medicines for every disease known to man. The man that my father sent along with me and keep me safe had spoken with the apothecary, who informed him that no amount of medicine would work on me. He suggested my caretaker bring me to the mountainside at the edge of Rome. Once we arrived, there was a dark cave. My caretaker left me just outside of it and told me he would return at first light of the morning. I stood there for a while, confused, but then I heard humming coming from inside. I wasn't sure at first if I should go in or not, but something drew me in. As I entered, all I saw was darkness, but the further I made my way in, I began to see candles lining the floors against the walls. The deeper I went, the more the candles and the brighter it got. Eventually, I reached a clearing and saw a woman standing at an altar. Without raising her head to look at me, she began to speak."

"*I've been waiting for you. Please come forward.*"

"I hesitated at first, but then I felt that pull again when she started speaking again."

"*Don't be afraid. I will not harm you. I am here to help you, Thibauld.*"

"I asked her how she knew my name, but she didn't answer, she just smiled. When I got closer to her, she moved from behind the altar and came around to me. She put her hand on my cheek and looked into my eyes."

"*You will suffer no more, my child.*"

"She slid her hand down to my shoulder and then walk around me, so she was at my back. She leaned forward to whisper in my ear."

"My name is Agatha. I am going to help you, and one day you will be called upon to help in a great battle."

"After she finished speaking, she sunk her teeth into me. The next thing I remembered, I woke as a vampire. The following morning, my caretaker came and brought me back to my father."

"What was his reaction?" Abigail asks.

"He didn't know how I was healed so quickly, and I didn't tell him, at least not at first. He was so happy that I had been *cured*, he decided to take me on trips around the world. He was afraid that there was still a chance the sickness could come back, and he wanted me to see as much as I could before that happened."

"I've always wanted to travel, where did you go? What have you seen?"

"Everything. Over the course of several years, we traveled from one place to another. Places like Peru, Brazil, Spain, Russia, Sweden, the Qing Dynasty, and even a bit of the Americas; finally making our way through Venice and ending in London before returning to our home in Paris."

"Sounds exotic," Abigail says. "But you mentioned that you didn't tell your father at first how you had healed so quickly. When did you tell him, and why?"

"You caught that, did you?"

"Of course I did," Abigail smirks.

"I didn't tell my father until we were back home from all of our travels. He had noticed that through the course of our trips, I had been getting stronger, and it was happening very quickly."

"Because you were feeding."

"Yes. When I first told him, he thought I had gone mad. He thought whatever medicine was given to me in Rome, had caused me to lose my mind. So, I had to prove to him that I was telling the truth. I made him one of us. Once he saw the power that came with it, he suggested that the Order should be for vampire kind. Should any Human come knocking with a hope to join our secret society, they would have to past a test."

"What kind of test?" asks Abigail.

"It was a ritual we referred to as a Bloodletting. The eight leaders of the order would gather around the new recruit. Each would sink their sharp teeth into the victim if he didn't survive the ritual; it meant he wasn't cut out to be part of us."

"Is that what happened to my father?" She inquires.

"Yes, I believe so." Thibauld replies taking a deep breath and exhales. "If only I were there, I could have stopped it. I would've known right away the transformation wouldn't take hold."

"What happened to you, Thibauld Devereux?"

"What do you mean, dearest Abigail?"

"I remembered how much of a scoundrel you were all those months ago on the roof, but the Thibauld before me now is not a scoundrel but a gentleman for the most part. So I say again, what happened to you, Thibauld Devereux?"

"That night on the roof, I was a scoundrel as you say, but when you fell to your death, and I watched your body hit the street below, I felt sick to my stomach," he says as he gently wraps both his hands around hers. "I thought I had lost you forever. I couldn't picture my life without you in it, and I would never be able to live with myself if you were harmed by my hand."

"What are you saying?" Abigail asks.

"Abigail I am, and always have been, madly in love with you. I know you can't love me the way I love you, but I need you in my life, and because I robbed you of your life, the least I can do is help you stop Collete and her revolution."

"Thibauld, I'm..I'm not sure what to say here." Abigail takes a deep breath, "I'm sorry, I just don't think right now is the time for us to discuss this. I do appreciate you honestly and your help with my mother, but there's one more thing I still don't understand."

Thibauld nods, "Okay, and what might your question be?"

"You said earlier that each one of us is granted a single gift at the time of our rebirth."

"Yes, that's correct." Thibauld replies.

"Then why do I have the ability of enhanced vision and the gift of foresight?"

"Have you experienced anything else?"

"Actually, now that I think about it, I think I may have the power of persuasion."

"Okay, so that is three, just like Collete. I find it intriguing that you both share persuasion as an ability."

"Okay, glad you're intrigued, but you still haven't answered my question."

"Oh, yes, of course. Sorry. The more abilities a vampire has, the stronger they are."

Abigail smiles, "So, that means I've stronger than you." She says and jabs him in the shoulder.

Thibauld furrows his brow.

"What? I'm just playing." Abigail says.

"No, it's not that."

"What is it then?" She asks.

"Well, I told you of my ability." He says.

"Yes. Strength."

"Yes. Well, because of it, I don't usually feel a punch unless some object is used to hit me other than a fist."

"Yes, and your point is?"

"Well, I think you may have a fourth ability because that jab, my dearest Abigail, was felt. If my ability is strength, then you, my dear, are much stronger than myself."

Abigail smiles again, "That must be very difficult for you to admit." Then she winks.

Thibauld smiles back, "If it were anyone else, I may have an issue, but you, my dearest Abigail, you can best me any time." He winks back at her. "Are you ready to face your mother?"

"Not yet."

"What do you need?"

"There's going to be at least two hundred people at the masquerade ball. We're going to need more for our side."

"I think I may have an idea."

"Okay. Please do tell."

"Jazmyne." Thibauld states.

Abigail looks confused, so he clarifies.

"I found her at the workhouse. We could send her back there to *recruit* more for our army."

Abigail thinks on it for a moment, "Yes. Do it. Send her there."

"Your wish is my command," Thibauld replies.

"And maybe Ansel can send for his uncle," Abigail suggests.

From the doorway, they hear Ansel, "Already done, madam. I sent for him a few days ago."

"Excellent," Thibauld states and claps his hands together.

Abigail kisses Ansel on the cheek, "Thank you. What would I ever do without you."

Chapter Nineteen

In the middle of the square, in front of Place De La Concorde, Marie Antoinette's execution is about to take place. Hidden amongst the crowd are Abigail, Thibauld, Ansel, and his uncle, the younglings, and the newest recruits from the warehouse standing with Jazmyne. Everyone is looking on, and Abigail notices Collete standing on a balcony observing the scene and leans into Thibauld.

"There she is." She whispers, and he nods.

A few moments later, they notice Collete disappears from the balcony and then reappears exiting the building. She makes a turn and begins walking.

"She's heading to the hotel for the ball," Abigail says.

"Okay, I will follow closely behind and stay in the shadows. Once we are both inside, I will be watching for your signal."

Abigail begins to follow her mother at a safe distance, being sure not to get her attention in any way. They had a plan, and that did not involve any kind of advancements in the middle of the street.

Periodically, Collete would stop, but she would never look around, she would just stand there as if she was listening for something. Then she would begin to walk again. Abigail kept her distance and stayed as quiet as she could. Her mother may have had the ability to make herself unseen, but Abigail has abilities of her own, and she knew how to go unnoticed. Ansel taught her how to be invisible during her training.

On the other side of the river, Hotel De Salm is beautiful. With vintage engravings, a pavilion, and center dome, this vast building just opened its doors three years earlier.

Abigail watches her mother enter and then takes a moment to appreciate its beauty before making her entrance. As the doormen open the doors for her to enter, she notices a string band playing and the attendees mingling with their drinks in hand. The music stops, and everyone in the room turns to face the young auburn-haired woman in her infinite beauty.

Abigail stands in her all-black gown, lace crossed at her neck. The dress flows gracefully from her waistline and is beaded with rhinestones. Underneath, no one can see that she is wearing boots that lace up her calves to her knees.

Only one man in the crowd is brave enough to approach. He extends his arm, taking Abigail's hand in his and leans over to gently kiss her knuckles.

"Good evening madam, I am Jacque Bisset. It's a pleasure to have you grace us with your presence on such a splendid occasion. Would you care to dance?"

"I'm Abigail, and I would love to dance, but it seems the band has stopped playing." replies the young woman.

Jacque raises his right hand, signaling the band to begin playing as they were before. This time the music was a soft romantic melody that would almost carry you across the dance floor without ever lifting or moving your feet.

Abigail and Jacque glide across the floor like two lovers dancing in the sheets. Everyone in the room watches them as if it's the first time witnessing such a perfect display of beauty radiating from the two of them. Jacque gestures to the crowd instructing they all mind their business and dance.

Abigail whispers softly into his ear as she rests her head on his shoulder.

"I have always been intrigued by a man who can command a room."

"And I, madam, have always been fascinated by a woman who can get everyone's attention just by walking through the door. Tell me, Abigail, what brings you to my party tonight?"

Abigail moves her head and places it on Jacques other shoulder; she again whispers in his ear. "I came to kill a vampire."

Jacque removes his mask; Abigail immediately recognizes him as the man from her dreams.

"Why do you think I sent you the invitation, if anyone can end Collete's reign, it would be you. That's why I saved you that night. I need you to save us all from the evils of the world."

The two of them continue dancing, and Abigail notices several men dressed in black hooded cloaks, the new members of the Order that Collete has *collected,* and one that is the sixth member she has been in search of. Then Jacque spins Abigail and dips her just as the song is ending. While she is held in the dip, she sees her mother standing on a staircase, closely watching their every move.

When Jacque lifts her back up to a standing position, she makes eye contact with Thibauld in the back of the room, and she nods her head ever so slightly, then looks at the sixth member. Thibauld nods back, acknowledging her signal. Then Abigail looks at Jacque straight in the eyes and says, "Your wish is granted."

He looks confused at first until he hears a shrill scream, and all attention is turned to Thibauld holding the head of the sixth of the eight members on Abigail's list, Reginald Laflamme, a politician.

Jacque looks back to Abigail, who is ripping off the skirt of her ballgown to reveal black leather pants with several weapons attached from her hips to her ankles; knives, stakes, and much more; all usually used as close-range weapons.

The main doors to the ballroom burst open, and a flood of younglings lead by Ansel, his uncle, Jazmyne and Artemis begin to attack the hooded members. All hell breaks loose, and the guests scramble in chaos to flee the scene and save their own necks. The unfortunate thing is, most of them are humans that Collete had invited herself with plans to feed on or turn later in the night. None of them were aware of the existence of vampires, and no one outside these walls knew of them either. Ansel and his uncle had to barricade the exits as no one would be allowed to leave this night as a human ever again. That is *if* they even survived the night.

Some of the younglings are holding their own, but others are being killed as if slicing a knife through butter. One by one, the hooded members are taken down, yet still, it seems there are so many; Collete has clearly been busy building an army of her own.

Abigail grabs one member from behind as they are reaching for Jazmyne, "I don't think so," she says as she uses one of the knives stashed at her hip to slice his throat.

Another hooded member grabs Abigail just as she releases the body of the one she just killed, but before they can do anything to her, Jacque places his hands on the man's temples and twist his head until he hears the crack of his neck being broken.

Abigail looks to Jacque and nods in surprise and appreciation. She then looks across the room and sees Ansel and his uncle, back to back, Ansel is holding a spear, while his uncle is using an iron-tipped stake. Each one, plunging the ends into their attackers. To the right of them a bit further away, Abigail sees Artemis swinging a sword as if he had been using it his whole life. Slicing the heads clear off those members surrounding him.

The sight and smell of the blood are intensifying the adrenaline surging through them all. Growls and screams of anger and rage can be heard as the fighting continues. The white marble flooring is now a river of red. Some guests are even slipping and losing their balance as they try to run for the exits. Others are being slaughtered in the wake of the battle.

Abigail fights off another member and uses her strength to pierce her hand through the man's chest and rips out his heart as it is still beating. As is body falls in front of her, she notices another hooded member is sneaking up behind Ansel. She grabs a dagger from her boot and sends it flying across the room and sticks into the man's throat.

Ansel looks at the man just as the dagger makes its mark, and then he looks to Abigail, smiles, and then nods.

Abigail then turns her attention to the staircase and notices her mother is gone. She searches the room while fighting off more. Looking to the left, then the right; nowhere is Collete to be found.

Abigail snarls in frustration.

Jacque hears her and turns his head slightly in her direction, and he maintains eye contact with his current attacker, "What's wrong?"

"She's gone! I can't see her anywhere."

At that moment, her attention is pulled away and drawn to a horrifying shriek.

"NO!" screams Jazmyne just as Ansel's uncle thrusts his weapon deep into the chest of Artemis mistakenly in all the chaos. It is forced in so deep it protrudes out his back.

"Oh, No!" Abigail exclaims.

Both women run to Artemis.

"I...I...I didn't mean to. I'm so sorry. There was so much confusion." Ansel's uncle tries to explain.

"This is all your fault!" Jazmyne yells at Abigail, "You are the one that insisted this battle had to take place! All we wanted was to leave and live a peaceful life far away from here, but he was so loyal to you and Thibauld! I will never forgive you for this, Abigail! Never!"

Jazmyne collapses on top of Artemis' body; she is consumed by grief and anger as tears stream down her face.

Then Abigail notices...aside from Jazmyne's crying, there is nothing but utter silence...then laughter.

Collete is standing on the staircase once again, and all eyes are on her.

"What's funny?" Abigail asks.

"Looks like you lose," Collete replies, "and you still have two original members left to kill. Can you guess who they are?"

"Clearly you, mother," Abigail replies.

"Yes, of course, and the other?" Collete prompts.

Abigail furrows her brow, "I know who the other is, but he no longer serves you."

"Is that so?" Collete retorts, "Well, in that case..." Without finishing her sentence, she uses her super-speed to advance on

Abigail in an attempt to end her life. But just as Collete appears in front of her ready to send an iron-tipped arrow through Abigail's eye, Thibauld moves in front of Abigail in an attempt to block the attack, and the arrow embeds itself through the side of his neck.

Before Collete can react, a chain is wrapped around her neck from behind. She grabs for it as it is choking her, but Ansel has a tight grip, and there is no give. As he is holding her in place, Abigail pulls a six-inch iron cross from inside her top and plunges it straight into her mother's heart. She then leans forward and places a kiss on her mother's cheek and whispers in her ear.

"For father...one less evil in this world."

As soon as Collete's body falls to the floor, Abigail turns her attention to Thibauld, rushing to his side.

Ansel's uncle is applying pressure on Thibauld's wound, trying to hold back the bleeding.

Abigail leans in, "Thibauld, why did you do that? You stupid, stupid man." A tear runs down her cheek.

"Anything for you, my dearest Abigail. I told you I loved you. Your life is much more important than my own."

Abigail places a passionate kiss on his lips as he begins to lose conciseness and slips away to his death.

After a moment, Jacque places his hands on her shoulders and coxes her to stand, then wraps her in his arms in comfort.

Ansel clears his throat, "Miss, there are still a lot of guests left alive here. Maybe a few words should be said before you decide what is to be done with them?" He suggests.

Abigail lifts her head from Jacque's chest, "Yes, yes, you're right."

She makes her way to the staircase and stands before everyone, "I know you are all scared and confused by what you have just witnessed. As it stands today, the outside world has no knowledge of our kind, and unfortunately for you all, it needs to remain that way. So, you have two choices. You either consent to becoming one of us, or you accept your fate of death, but these doors will not be opened until one or the other is complete."

A voice speaks from the group, "what if everyone in this room pledges their loyalty to you? Would you let us go without changing us or killing us? Wouldn't that show a step of good faith on your part to bring peace between humans and vampires?"

Abigail looks to Ansel and Jacque, who both nod showing they will accept whatever decision she makes.

"Yes. I believe that would be acceptable."

Everyone bows and makes their pledge, and with an agreement in place, Ansel and his uncle open the doors for everyone to leave.

As Jazmyne begins to walk out, she stops, turns, and then glares at Abigail, "You will never have my loyalty again." Then she disappears out into the night.

Chapter Twenty

Back at Abigail's, Abigail, Jacque, and the younglings are settling in, in the living room, and Ansel is bringing them all tea.

"How are you doing, Miss?" Ansel asks as he hands Abigail a cup of tea. "It can't have been easy killing your own mother."

Jacque walks over and places a hand on Abigail's shoulder.

"Yes. We are all concerned for you, my dear; you've also lost a good friend. How are you holding up?"

"I will be okay. Thibauld was a long-time friend, and I will miss him, but he wouldn't want me to mourn him for long. As far as my mother, it does break my heart that she was so evil, but her rein needed to end, and fate decided I was the one who had to do it. Our world would have been destroyed if she managed to survive, and I just could let that happen."

"Well, we are all so grateful that she will not be here to follow through with her plans." Jacque states.

"Yes." Abigail agrees.

"So what's next?" one of the younglings chime in.

Abigail turns her attention to the seven remaining younglings who survived the battle. She pauses for a moment and then takes a deep breath.

"We, all of us, need to make sure that our existence remains hidden from humans. I will be assigning you each to a region. Jacque, Ansel, and I will stay in the North region, the rest of you will disperse to the Northeast, East, Southeast, South, Southwest, West, and Northwest."

Everyone nods in agreement.

Abigail takes Jacque by the hand and leads him out of the room into the hallway.

"I've seen you in my dreams." Says Abigail. "I'm not sure why, but I can't get you out of my head even though this is our first official meeting. Why did you save me that night? Would you have done the same thing for anyone else?"

"To be perfectly honest, I have been keeping an eye on you for several years. On the night of my rebirth, the woman who changed me said I should keep you close until the time is right. I wasn't sure why, but when I saw you fall from the roof, I knew it was time."

"Who was this woman?"

"I'm not sure I had never met her before, nor did I see her again after, but I did ask her name," Jacque replies.

"And the name the woman gave? what was it?" Abigail asks.

"Agatha"

One Month Later...

In the village of Versailles, Abigail, in her white slip, walks barefoot by the stream. She listens to the sounds of the whistling winds and the chirping of birds in the early evening sun. As she walks across the moist grass, she hears a humming from behind the trees.

"Hello, is there anybody there?" She asks.

"Yes. I'm here." Says Jacque as he steps out from behind the tree.

"You seem a bit overdressed for a stroll through the forest, Sir," Remarks Abigail with a smile as she observes his waistcoat.

"And you, madam, have nothing to protect your feet, it seems we're both out of our element on this fine evening," Jacque replies with a grin.

"Where are you from? I haven't seen you around here before."

"No madam, I suspect you wouldn't have. I've only just arrived a few days ago. This is the first chance I've had to explore this little village of yours."

"Oh, Jacque," Abigail says with a grin. "I tire of this game, let us go inside.

"As you wish, my dearest Abigail." He says, gently grabbing her hand.

The young couple walks back through the woods and returns to Collete's château where they now live.

Epilogue

July 9, 1935: Kings Cross Train Station, London, England.

A scrawny twig of a man named Micheal Clifton deboards a train and collects his bags from the platform. Micheal is a writer who has been traveling the globe in the hopes of proving myths and monsters are real, and they are living among us. When he heard stories about a 158-year-old vampire protecting the cobblestone streets of London, he immediately packed his bags and left the United States. Upon his arrival at the kings crossing train station, a very tall, well-built mysterious man in a long black coat and fedora hat greeted Micheal.

"Pardon me, sir." the mysterious man asks. "Are you, Mr. Clifton?"

"Yes," Micheal says with a look of confusion as he pulls a filterless cigarette from his pants pocket, he lights it with a silver Zippo lighter and places the lighter back in his pocket. *(This is my first time in London, I have never been out of the United States).* He thought to himself. *(How could anyone know that I'm here. I've only just arrived here a few minutes ago.)*

"What can I do for you, Sir?" Micheal asks.

"My name is Geoffrey Perretti, and my employer would like you to come with me. I was instructed to meet you here and have you follow me."

"Why would I do that?" Micheal replies, "Who is your employer?"

Geoffrey reaches into his inside coat pocket and clenches his fist. After pulling his hand back from inside the coat, he holds out his fist toward Micheal. Micheal holds his hand out flat. The long-coated man opens his fist and drops a wrought iron cross necklace into Micheal's hand.

"She said you would know what this was as soon as you lay eyes on it."

"Yes. She was correct, lead the way," Micheal says with a smile. A short time later, Micheal and Geoffrey arrive at the steps of a lavish mansion. Geoffrey ascends the front steps and approaches the door. He turns the knob and pushes it open, then gestures for Micheal to follow him. As Micheal enters the building, he's stunned by the beautiful interior. At the entrance, you were greeted by a grand staircase, and a crystal chandelier hung from the ceiling above. As they furthered their way into the dimly lit mansion, Micheal takes notice of a writing desk in the foyer. It reminded him of the one he had back home in his Chicago apartment. Geoffrey leads Micheal into the parlor. He sees two chairs facing a fireplace with their backs toward Micheal. He can see the top of a woman's head as she sits in front of the fire. The flames crackle and the wood pops as it burns.

"Glad you could join me, Mr. Clifton." says the woman in the chair. I trust you had a restful journey from the states?"

"Yes. It was quite relaxing." Micheal responds. "Now, can someone tell me what I'm doing here?"

"Your name is Micheal Clifton, and for the last few years, you have been traveling the world in search of myths, legends, and monsters. Is that about right?"

"Yes. I'm a journalist in search of a story. I can feel it in my heart that the evils of the world are real and are hiding in plain sight. I believe it to be a story that needs to be told." he replies. "Now, madam, if you please, Who exactly are you?"

"My name is Abigail Cariveau." She says as she stands to her feet and gestures toward the other chair. "Sit down, Mr. Clifton. I have one hell of a story to tell you.

Abigail's story continues in:

Out for Blood

An Abigail Cariveau Story

About the Author

Born in North Carolina, raised in Florida.
Inspired by John Connelly, Sir Arthur
Conan Doyle, and horror writers like
Stephen King.